D0604027

The
Little
Big
Book
of
Cats

The Little Big Book of Cats

Edited by ALICE WONG and LENA TABORI

Designed by TIMOTHY SHANER
AND CHRISTOPHER MEASOM

welcome
BOOKS

NEW YORK • SAN FRANCISCO

Published in 2005 by Welcome Books®
An imprint of Welcome Enterprises, Inc.
6 West 18th Street, New York, NY 10011
(212) 989-3200; Fax (212) 989-3205
www.welcomebooks.com

Publisher: Lena Tabori   Project Director: Alice Wong
Designers: Timothy Shaner and Christopher Measom
Project Assistants: Kate DeWitt and Jeffrey McCord
Cat Tales retold by Deidra Garcia
Living with Cats, Cats Training, Fun and Games, and Kitty Treats text by Ellen Leach

Front jacket illustration by D. Merlin

Library of Congress Cataloging-in-Publication Data on file.

ISBN-10: 1-932183-80-9
ISBN-13: 978-1-932183-80-1

Printed in China

FIRST EDITION

3 5 7 9 10 8 6 4 2

Contents

Poetry

Training and Tricks

Contents

Fun and Games

Kitty Treats

Feline Funnies

Foreword

My mother is afraid of all things furry. My only childhood consolation was that someday, I would have as many furry creatures as I wanted. Of course, I married a man who is allergic to cats. I joke with him that after he passes, I will become an old lady with lots of cats! In the meantime, I see my in-laws' barn cat on weekends. Red is a one-on-one cat, very particular about who is the "one." I love that about him. Most cats force you to work for their trust. Red will appear when I'm alone, hoping for a good brushing or massage. He'll sit beside me on an outdoor bench and enjoy the sun. He'll wait for me on top of the fence for a good-night scratch. At the first hint of another human's presence, he is gone.

These complex creatures have inspired countless great writers and poets. You might find that many of the selections in this volume are longer than usual in our Little Big Books. The cat simply requires more words to capture. I could not bear to shorten Charles Dudley Warner's account of his majestic cat Calvin, or any more of Alice Adams's description of the lovely Lily. I am certain that cat lovers know how to appreciate and savor a good, long read.

Much of the original text in this book is by Ellen Leach, my cat consultant and a great cat lover . . . *she* has had a *lot* of cats. The trick was to present the right amount of information with a bit of fun. So you will find cat training and cat care here, but also cat games, recipes, and feline funnies! Then there is the art. Selecting good, interesting, and varied works from among the vintage cat illustrations available was a difficult task, but I think we have succeeded . . . the illustrations, and the book, are fabulous. Enjoy.   —ALICE WONG

Ever since my toddlerhood, our house had paw prints on every surface. Teeming with birds, fish, dogs, hamsters, guinea pigs, turtles, and horned toads, it was a project in animal accumulation.

Our first was a black-and-white tuxedo stray I found next to our yard at the age of two and a half. I half dragged, half carried the kitten to my mother. She wasn't pleased, but the tiny ball of fluff did not grant right of refusal. Named Kitty because no other name would stick, his favorite activity was lying in the middle of our Ping-Pong table during a game. He would often "assist."

In these pages, you'll discover what animal lovers know: If the lion is king of the jungle, then the house cat is king of the castle. Far more intelligent than people give them credit for, cats are challenging, fun, and highly trainable—on their terms, of course. Once you begin to interact seriously with them, amazement and wonder are sure to follow.

Thanks go to Linus and Phoebe, two clicker-trained Burmese whose copy-editing and computer-mouse-chasing abilities have proved invaluable. I would also like to thank Kitty, Toi, Ming, Midas, Seesha, Rosebud, Muji, Wysiwig, and all my other friends who wait for me "across the Rainbow Bridge."   —ELLEN LEACH

If man could be crossed with the cat, it would improve man, but deteriorate the cat.

— MARK TWAIN

Macavity— The Mystery Cat

by T. S. Eliot

Macavity's a Mystery Cat: he's called the Hidden Paw—
For he's the master criminal who can defy the Law.
He's the bafflement of Scotland Yard, the Flying Squad's despair:
For when they reach the scene of crime—*Macavity's not there!*

Macavity, Macavity, there's no one like Macavity,
He's broken every human law, he breaks the law of gravity.
His powers of levitation would make a fakir stare,
And when you reach the scene of crime—*Macavity's not there!*
You may seek him in the basement, you may look up in the air—
But I tell you once and once again, *Macavity's not there!*

Macavity's a ginger cat, he's very tall and thin;
You would know him if you saw him, for his eyes are sunken in.
His brow is deeply lined with thought, his head is highly domed;
His coat is dusty from neglect, his whiskers are uncombed.
He sways his head from side to side, with movements like a snake;
And when you think he's half asleep, he's always wide awake.

Macavity, Macavity, there's no one like Macavity,
For he's a fiend in feline shape, a monster of depravity.
You may meet him in a by-street, you may see him in the square—
But when a crime's discovered, then *Macavity's not there!*

He's outwardly respectable. (They *say* he cheats at cards.)
And his footprints are not found in any file of Scotland Yard's.
And when the larder's looted, or the jewel-case is rifled,
Or when the milk is missing, or another Peke's been stifled,
Or the greenhouse glass is broken, and the trellis past repair—
Ay, there's the wonder of the thing! *Macavity's not there!*

And when the Foreign Office finds a Treaty's gone astray,
Or the Admiralty lose some plans and drawings by the way,
There may be a scrap of paper in the hall or on the stair—
But it's useless to investigate—*Macavity's not there!*
And when the loss has been disclosed, the Secret Service say:
"It must have been Macavity!"—but he's a mile away.
You'll be sure to find him resting, or a-licking of his thumbs,
Or engaged in doing complicated long division sums.

Macavity, Macavity, there's no one like Macavity,
There never was a Cat of such deceitfulness and suavity.
He always has an alibi, and one or two to spare:
And whatever time the deed took place—MACAVITY WASN'T THERE!
And they say that all the Cats whose wicked deeds are widely known
(I might mention Mungojerrie, I might mention Griddlebone)
Are nothing more than agents for the Cat who all the time
Just controls their operations: the Napoleon of Crime!

Adopting a Cat

Think seriously about whether your lifestyle and budget can accommodate a pet. Cats are creatures of routine and require a stable living environment, regular care, and affection. If you've never owned a cat before, be sure to pick up a book or pamphlet on their care. Make sure you can afford the kind of monetary and emotional commitment it takes to become a companion to a furry child who can live to be 15 or even 20 years old.

There are organizations, including the American Society for the Protection of Animals (ASPCA), Humane Society, Bide-A-Wee, and local pet rescue groups, that will defray the costs of spaying, neutering, and vaccinations. In addition, these organizations often run clinics that provide discounted vet care. Consider adopting an abandoned animal from a shelter.

If you have your heart set on a purebred, be sure to contact a reputable breeder with checkable references and certification through the Cat Fanciers' Association (CFA) or the International Cat Association (TICA). In addition to the cute kittens you see at the cattery, consider adopting a full-grown cat who is being "retired." These often young show-quality adults have done their stints in the breeding and show circuits, and make terrific pets. An older cat can be a kinder, gentler companion.

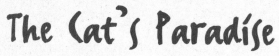

The Cat's Paradise

by Emile Zola

I was then two years old, and was at the same time the fattest and most naive cat in existence. At that tender age I still had all the presumptuousness of an animal who is disdainful of the sweetness of home.

How fortunate I was, indeed, that providence had placed me with your aunt! That good woman adored me. I had at the bottom of a wardrobe a veritable sleeping salon, with feather cushions and triple covers. My food was equally excellent; never just bread, or soup, but always meat, carefully chosen meat.

Well, in the midst of all this opulence, I had only one desire, one dream, and that was to slip out of the upper window and escape on to the roofs. Caresses annoyed me, the softness of my bed nauseated me, and I was so fat that it was disgusting even to myself. In short, I was bored the whole day long just with being happy.

I must tell you that by stretching my neck a bit, I had seen the roof directly in front of my window. That day four cats were playing with each other up there; their fur bristling, their tails high, they were romping around with every indication of joy on the blue roof slates baked by the sun. I had never before watched such an extraordinary spectacle. And from then on I had a definitely fixed belief: out there on that roof was true happiness, out there beyond the window which was always closed so carefully. In proof of that contention I remembered that the doors of the chest in which the meat was kept were also closed, just as carefully!

I resolved to flee. After all

there had to be other things in life besides a comfortable bed. Out there was the unknown, the ideal. And then one day they forgot to close the kitchen window. I jumped out on to the small roof above it.

How beautiful the roofs were! The wide eaves bordering them exuded delicious smells. Carefully I followed those eaves, where my feet sank into the fine mud that smelled tepid and infinitely sweet. It felt as if I were walking on velvet. And the sun shone with a good warmth that caressed my plumpness.

I will not hide from you the fact that I was trembling all over. There was something overwhelming in my joy. I remember particularly the tremendous emotional upheaval which actually made me lose my footing on the slates, when three cats rolled down from the ridge of the roof and approached with excited miaows. But when I showed signs of fear, they told me I was a silly fat goose and insisted that their miaowing was only laughter.

I decided to join them in their caterwauling. It was fun, even though the three stalwarts weren't as fat as I was and made fun of me when I rolled like a ball over the roof heated by the sun.

An old tomcat belonging to the gang honored me particularly with his friendship. He offered to take care of my education, an offer which I accepted with gratitude.

Oh, how far away seemed all the soft things of your aunt! I drank from the gutters, and never did sugared milk taste half as fine! Everything was good and beautiful.

A female cat passed by, a ravishing she, and the very sight of her filled me with strange emotions. Only in my dreams had I up to then seen such an exquisite creature with such a magnificently arched back. We dashed forward to meet the newcomer, my three companions

and myself. I was actually ahead of the others in paying the enchanting female my compliments; but then one of my comrades gave me a nasty bite in the neck, and I let out a shriek of pain.

"Pshaw!" said the old tomcat, dragging me away. "You will meet plenty of others."

After a walk that lasted an hour I had a ravenous appetite.

"What does one eat on these roofs?" I asked my friend the tom.

"Whatever one finds," he replied laconically.

This answer embarrassed me somewhat for, hunt as I might, I couldn't find a thing. Finally I looked through a dormer window and saw a young workman preparing his breakfast. On the table, just above the windowsill, lay a

chop of a particularly succulent red.

"There is my chance," I thought, rather naively.

So I jumped on to the table and snatched the chop. But the working-

man saw me and gave me a terrific wallop across my back with a broom. I dropped the meat, cursed rather vulgarly and escaped.

"What part of the world do you come from?" asked the tom-

21

The Cat's Paradise

cat. "Don't you know that meat on tables is meant only to be admired from afar? What we've got to do is look in the gutters."

I have never been able to understand why kitchen meat shouldn't belong to cats. My stomach began to complain quite bitterly. The tom tried to console me by saying it would only be necessary to wait for the night. Then, he said, we would climb down from the roofs into the streets and forage in the garbage heaps.

Wait for the night! Confirmed philosopher that he was, he said it calmly while the very thought of such a protracted fast made me positively faint.

Night came ever so slowly, a misty night that made me shiver. To make things worse, rain began to fall, a thin, penetrating rain whipped up by brisk howling gusts of wind.

How desolate the streets looked to me! There was noth-ing left of the good warmth, of the big sun, of those roofs where one could play so pleasantly. My paws slipped on the slimy pavement, and I began to think with some longing of my triple covers and my feather pillow.

We had hardly reached the street when my friend, the tom, began to tremble. He made himself small, quite small, and glided surreptitiously along the walls of the houses, warning me under his breath to be quick about it. When we reached the shelter of a house door, he hid behind it and purred with satisfaction. And when I asked him the reason for his strange conduct, he said:

"Did you see that man with the hook and the basket?"

"Yes."

"Well, if he had seen us, we would have been caught, fried on the spit and eaten!"

"Fried on the spit and eaten!" I exclaimed. "Why, then the

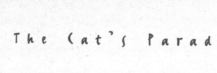

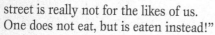

street is really not for the likes of us. One does not eat, but is eaten instead!"

In the meantime, however, they had begun to put the garbage out on the sidewalks. I inspected it with growing despair. All I found there were two or three dry bones that had obviously been thrown in among the ashes. And then and there I realized how succulent a dish of fresh meat really is!

My friend, the tom, went over the heaps of garbage with consummate artistry. He made me rummage around until morning, inspecting every cobblestone, without the least trace of hurry. But after ten hours of almost incessant rain my whole body was trembling. Damn the street, I thought, damn liberty! And how I longed for my prison!

When day came, the tomcat noticed that I was weakening.

"You've had enough, eh?" he asked in a strange voice.

"Oh, yes," I replied.

"Do you want to go home?"

"I certainly do. But how can I find my house?"

"Come along. Yesterday morning when I saw you come out I knew immediately that a cat as fat as you isn't made for the joys of liberty. I know where you live. I'll take you back to your door."

He said this all simply enough, the good, dignified tom. And when we finally got there, he added, without the slightest show of emotion:

"Goodbye, then."

"No, no!" I protested. "I shall not leave you like this. You come with me! We shall share bed and board. My mistress is a good woman . . ."

He didn't even let me finish.

"Shut up!" he said brusquely. "You are a fool. I'd die in that stuffy softness. Your abundant life is for weaklings. Free cats will never buy your comforts and your featherbeds at the price of being imprisoned. Goodbye!"

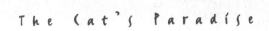

With these words he climbed back on to the roof. I saw his proud thin shadow shudder deliciously as it began to feel the warmth of the morning sun.

When I came home your aunt acted the martinet and administered a corrective which I received with profound joy. I reveled in being punished and voluptuously warm. And while she cuffed me, I thought with delight of the meat she would give me directly afterwards.

You see—an afterthought, while stretched out before the embers—true happiness, paradise, my master, is where one is locked up and beaten, wherever there is meat.

I speak for cats.

Hide-and-Seek for Treats

Ever wonder if you can teach your cat to come? Well, you can! All you need to do is teach her to associate her name with rewards, by treating consistently. Hide-and-Seek for Treats conditions the cat to come when alerted. (Think of it as "You've got food!" instead of "You've got mail!").

a human helper, one or more feline "hound dogs," a few of your cat's favorite (smelly) treats

1. Have your helper take the cat (or cats) into a closed room. (This alone will pique her interest; cats are always on the wrong side of a closed door.) Your assistant should count slowly to 100 while you hide in a closet, under a bed, or in another place. (Don't go up the ladder into the attic at first; increase the difficulty later.)

2. Release the cat.

3. Reward your cat with a treat as soon as she finds you. If she seems to give up, say pssst! or make some scratching sounds to teach her the game.

4. Repeat the above steps, choosing a new location. If you are behind a closet door, poke the treat out from under it when your cat locates you.

5. Once you've played a few rounds and your cat understands the game, add a cue. Rap the floor twice and say "Come!" as she is on her way to you. She will eventually associate this cue with you and the treats.

What's a cat's favorite dessert?
Chocolate mousse.

What happened to the cat who
swallowed a ball of yarn?
She had mittens.

What do cat actors say on stage?
Tabby or not tabby!

What did the cat say when
he lost all his money?
I'm paw.

What's the unluckiest kind
of cat to have?
A catastrophe!

Why did the cat join the Red Cross?
Because she wanted to be a first-aid kit.

What is the name of the unauthorized
autobiography of the cat?
Hiss and Tell.

Is it bad luck if a black cat follows you?
That depends on whether you're a man or a mouse.

If a cat is a flabby tabby, then
what is a very small cat?
An itty bitty kitty.

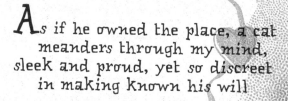

As if he owned the place, a cat
   meanders through my mind,
sleek and proud, yet so discreet
   in making known his will

that I hear music when he mews,
   and even when he purrs
a tender timbre in the sound
   compels my consciousness—

a secret rhythm penetrates
   to unsuspected depths,
obsessive as a line of verse
   and potent as a drug:

all woes are spirited away,
   I hear ecstatic news—
it seems a telling language has
   no need of words at all.

My heart, assenting instrument,
   is masterfully played;
no other bow across its strings
   can draw such music out

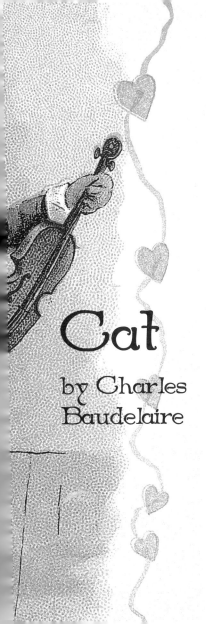

Cat

by Charles Baudelaire

the way this cat's uncanny voice
    —seraphic, alien—
can reconcile discordant strains
    into close harmony!

One night his brindled fur gave off
    a perfume so intense
I seemed to be embalmed because
    just once! I fondled him . . .

Familiar spirit, genius, judge,
    the cat presides—inspires
events that he appears to spurn,
    half goblin and half god!

and when my spellbound eyes at last
    relinquish worship of
this cat they love to contemplate
    and look inside myself,

I find to my astonishment
    like living opals there
his fiery pupils, embers which
    observe me fixedly.

Dogs and Cats

by Pierre Loti

Cats are possessed of a shy, retiring nature, cajoling, haughty, and capricious, difficult to fathom. They reveal themselves only to certain favored individuals, and are repelled by the faintest suggestion of insult or even by the most trifling deception.

They are quite as intelligent as dogs, and are devoid of the yielding obsequiousness, the ridiculous sense of importance, and the revolting coarseness of these latter animals. Cats are dainty patricians, whereas dogs, whatever their social status, retain a *parvenu's* lack of cleanliness, and are irredeemably vulgar.

A cat is watching me. . . . He is close at hand, on the table, and thrusts forward his dimly thoughtful little head, into which some unwonted flash of intelligence has evidently just entered. Whilst servants or visitors have been on the spot, he has scornfully kept out of the way, under an armchair, for no other person than myself is allowed to stroke his invariably immaculate coat. But no sooner does he perceive that I am alone than he comes and sits in front of me, suddenly assuming one of those expressive looks that are seen from time to time in such enigmatical, contemplative

animals as belong to the same genus as himself. His yellow
eyes look up at me, wide open, the pupils dilated by a men-
tal effort to interrogate and attempt to understand: "Who
are you, after all?" he asks. "Why do I trust you? Of
what importance are you in the world?
What are you thinking and doing here?"

In our ignorance of things, our inability
to know anything, how amazing—perhaps
terrifying—if we could but see into the curi-
ous depths of those eyes and fathom the *unknowable* within
the little brain hidden away there! Ah! if only for a moment
we could put ourselves in its place and afterwards remember, what an instantaneous and definite solution—though
no doubt terrifying enough—we might obtain of the perplex-
ing problems of life and eternity! Are these familiar animals
our inferiors and far removed from us, or are they terribly
near to us? Is the dark veil which conceals from them the
cause and end of life more dense than that stretched before
our own eyes? . . . No, never will it be our privilege to solve
the secret of those little wheedling heads, which allow
themselves so lovingly to be held and stroked, almost
crushed, in our hands. . . .

And now he is about to sleep, maybe to dream, on this
table at which I am writing; he settles down as close to me
as possible, after stretching out his paw towards me two or

three times, looking at me as though craving permission to leap on to my knees. And there he lies, his head daintily resting on my arm, as though to say: "Since you will not have me altogether, permit this at least, for I shall not disturb you if I remain so."

How mysterious is the *affection* of animals! It denotes something lofty, something superior in those natures about which we know so little.

And how well I can understand Mohammed, who, in response to the chant of the *muezzin* summoning him to prayers, cut off with a pair of scissors the hem of his cloak before rising to his feet, for fear of disturbing his cat, which had settled down thereon to sleep.

Clicker Training Step I
To Begin

How do animal trainers get cats in the movies and TV commercials to do such amazing things on cue? "Cats are impossible for me to train!" you say. Discover what the pros have known for years: a) It's not really "training"; b) you can't ask for something without paying for it; and c) all you need is a clicker and treats.

Forget command and obedience. Think that cats are independent? Well, you're wrong: They are union members, and they want to get paid for their work. It's a silent union, but a powerful one. If they feel their pay has been unfairly docked, then they will go on strike, ignoring you, exchanging looks of disdain with their comrades, and stalking off with tails and heads held high. But if you are fair, they'll be willing partners in the clicker game.

Do you have a cat who shreds the toilet paper, overturns the wastebaskets, and trashes your home on his wild rampages? Many of these undesirable behaviors are simply the result of the boredom of being housebound and getting too little interaction. Does he hide under the bed foaming at the mouth when the carrier comes out, and would you like him to learn to be "self-

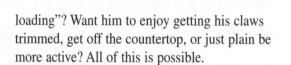

Step I: To Begin

loading"? Want him to enjoy getting his claws trimmed, get off the countertop, or just plain be more active? All of this is possible.

First: Buy a Clicker

Clicker training, based on the science of operant conditioning, is so popular nowadays that you can buy clickers at any number of outlets. The sharp, precise sound of the click "marks" a behavior and signals to an animal's subconscious that she has done something right and a treat is coming. It's needed as a marker because of the timing issue: You cannot get the reward to the animal fast enough to correctly signal what it is she did right. You also can't clap your hands or say "Yes!" fast enough or sharply enough, and since these are sounds heard

37

Step I: To Begin

outside of training, too, they serve only to confuse your student.

Look for a clicker that emits a soft click for a cat's sound-sensitive ears, or use tape to pad a dog clicker. You can find one at your local pet supply shop or on the Internet.

Second: Practice

First, do not click your clicker near your cat's face, or near any-one's ear, for that matter. Your first session happens without the cat and is all about timing. Close yourself off in a room, sit in front of the TV, and try to click whenever you think a character is going to begin speaking. Practice clicking AS the actor opens his or her mouth, not after. You will need to be able to click during a behavior—this is harder than you think.

Third: "Charge" the Clicker

Introduce the clicker to your cat. At first, you will be using your pet's absolute favorite (preferably smelly) treat—cheese, bits of meat, human-grade tuna, peanuts—all chopped into extremely small bits, each smaller than a pea. Commercial treats may not be best, but if you use these, break each one into four or five pieces. The cat has to be able to eat each treat very quickly. This

Step 1: To Begin

works for one cat or more, but you may have your hands full treating a group!

The next part is easy: Click, and hand her a treat. If she tries to steal the treats, hold them up out of the way; use a plate if they're really messy. Try to get your cat to take the treat directly from your fingers or a cupped hand; if this doesn't work, simply toss it on the floor. Wait till she downs the first bit, and then click and treat again.

If your cat walks away, let her—she either is not hungry, doesn't like your choice of treat, or is distracted. Click, hold the treat out, and wait for her to return. Don't call her or make noises. Click and treat for 20 or so repeats. By this time, the cat will understand that the click means food is coming.

Congratulations! You're on your way.

Catnip Snaps

When kitty decides that maybe he's not in the mood for his breakfast, entice him with a treat or two to start his engines. Try these tempting homemade treats to rev up your little prince or princess.

1/2 cup soy flour
3/4 cup whole wheat flour
1 1/2 teaspoons catnip
2 tablespoons wheat germ
1/3 cup powdered milk
dash salt
1 tablespoon unsulphured molasses
1 egg
2 tablespoons butter
1/3 cup cat milk (Whiskas or other brand)

1. Preheat oven to 350°F.
2. Mix together dry ingredients.
3. Add molasses, egg, butter, and milk. Mix well.
4. Mixture will be sticky. The secret to working with it is to keep wet-ting your rolling pin and knife. Roll it out flat onto a greased cookie sheet. Use a little extra flour if it's too sticky. With a small knife, score into very small, treat-size pieces.
5. Bake for about 15 minutes, or until crisp and brown around the edges. Let cool, break apart, and store in a sealed container in the refrigerator. Keeps for about a week.

Makes about 250 training-size treats.

The Cat Life Cycle

You may have heard people say that cats and dogs live six or seven of their years for every one of ours. It turns out though, that an 18-month-old cat is already a grown-up. Cats mature at a rate of 15 to 1 compared to us during their first year, 10 to 1 during their second year, and then approximately 4 "human years" for every year after that.

"Terrible Twos" At four weeks, kittens are like tiny toddlers (except that they can run!)—ready to explore the world but able to sit in the palm of a hand. Young kittens should be fed kitten food, which is higher in protein than adult cat food, four times per day. Discuss your kitten's diet with your vet when you take your eight-week-old for his first shots (if he has not already been vaccinated).

Adolescent Urges At six months, a cat is usually about three-quarters of his adult weight (purebreds take a little longer to mature). Like teenagers, they are holy terrors, too—literally bouncing off walls and everything in between. Vets and animal welfare organizations recommend neutering by this time. After six months, an unneutered male will not hesitate to apply his personal "perfume" to his territory—and that includes your sofa, carpets, and clothing! And spaying is simple if done at four months, before your female's first heat.

Voting Age At a little over a year, your cat is like that energetic 19-year-old you just sent off to college: years of education, but not necessarily the best judgment. Your Grimalkin will spend the next few years in her prime, perfecting her athletic skills and developing her distinct markings.

The Middle-Aged Cat Age 6 to 10 is a wonderful time when cats still play

like youngsters but have learned a thing or two. You may notice some thickening fat pads around the ribs (your cat's, not yours!) by about age six. Now is the time to discuss your flabby tabby with your vet. Middle age also is a good time to consider a veterinary dental cleaning.

The Senior Cat By age 10, Puss achieves the height of his dignity. Most cats seem unfazed by a little arthritis, and deal with it by stretching. Your sen-

ior likes plenty of warmth. Make him feel like he's vacationing in Mexico by treating him to a heated pet bed or a pad made of special material designed to reflect his body heat. Pamper your older pet with a gentle massage (page 276). Reduced kidney function and thyroid problems are two common issues of old age. Veterinarians often request a broad panel of lab tests on one small blood sample to screen for numerous problems all at once.

A cat in distress,
Nothing more, nor less;
Good folks, I must faithfully tell ye,
As I am a sinner,
It waits for some dinner,
To stuff out its own little belly.

You would not easily guess
All the modes of distress
Which torture the tenants of earth;
And the various evils,
Which, like so many devils,
Attend the poor souls from their birth.

Some living require,
And other desire
An old fellow out of the way;
And which is best
I leave to be guessed,
For I cannot pretend to say.

One wants society,
Another variety,
Others a tranquil life;
Some want food,
Others, as good,
Only want a wife.

But this poor little cat
Only wanted a rat,
To stuff out its own little maw;
And it were as good
Some people had such food,
To make them *hold their jaw!*

Verses
on a Cat

by Percy Bysshe Shelley

A mouse in the paws is worth two in the pantry.

—LOUIS WAIN

CAT TALES

Many people know the story of Noah and the Ark—How it rained for 40 days and 40 nights, and the only thing that was saved on the planet was Noah, his family, and two of every creature created on the earth. But what may surprise you is that there was an animal that stepped off the Ark, that which had not originally stepped on. It was created by Noah on that strange journey, and this is how it came to be.

One More on the Ark

An Ancient Legend

As the rain poured down, and the currents pushed the mighty Ark from here to there, Noah's family came to him with a problem.

"Noah," his wife complained, "you have to do something about these rats. They are getting out of hand. All day long they nibble at the food supply, and all night long they scurry all over the deck. No one has gotten a decent meal or night's sleep since the rains began to fall!"

Noah knew this to be true, but he didn't know how to remedy the situation. He stroked his beard and told them, "I cannot raise my hand against a creature on this Ark. God has willed that they must arrive in the New Land unharmed."

CAT TALES

His family was not happy with this reply, and Noah fell asleep in very bad spirits. That night, he had a strange dream. He dreamed that he took one of his wife's hair combs and gently combed the fur on the lion's back. The more he combed, the more fur seemed to come off, and when Noah blew on the pile, it took form. But just as he was about to see what it would become, he woke up.

"What an odd dream," he mused. "Perhaps it was a message from God."

Although he felt slightly foolish, Noah set off to find the lion, his wife's comb in hand. When he found the great beast, he began combing the lion's back. As in the dream, more and more fur came off the golden cat as it yawned placidly, until finally a little pile was formed. Noah blew on the pile of fur, and suddenly, it took shape and meowed!

The family was delighted with the curious little creature, but they weren't quite sure why Noah had created it. "It is a beautiful animal," his wife admitted, "but does she do more than rumble like an earthquake and stroke her head against us?"

At that precise moment, one of the rats ran by with a piece of food in its mouth. The mysterious creature took one look at the rat and sprang

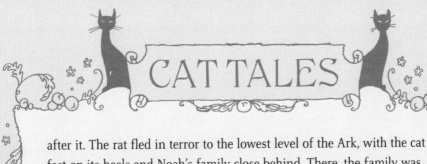

CAT TALES

after it. The rat fled in terror to the lowest level of the Ark, with the cat fast on its heels and Noah's family close behind. There, the family was horrified to discover that the rat had managed to gnaw a hole right in the side of the boat, and water was slowly trickling in.

"What will happen to us?" one of Noah's sons cried. "We will sink!"

Luckily for everyone, a brave little frog had witnessed this crisis, and leapt straight into the hole, plugging it with his small body. Noah was so grateful to the tiny creature that he made the frog amphibious, that is, able to live on the land and the water.

Meanwhile, the rat fled to a hiding place and remained there until the end of the journey.

The family was overjoyed at having the rat chased away. Noah picked up the lovely creature he had created and stroked her delicate head.

"From now on," Noah decided, "this will be called a cat. And she will be a companion to all people and welcomed in homes everywhere."

And she has been, ever since.

Scavenger Hunt

A Scavenger Hunt is a simple game that can involve the entire household and is hilarious to watch. It teaches your cat to depend on his sniffer—not just his eyes—to find prey objects. Stimulate your cat's "schnoz potential" by using extra-smelly treats at first. Do this before a mealtime, when Puff's a little hungry.

delicious treats, a food-oriented puss with a good sniffer

1. Close the cat in a room. Give him one tiny favorite treat to get him interested.
2. If the treats are messy, use small paper plates; otherwise, break dry treats into tiny bits. Place each bit in an obscure location: behind the TV or a wastebasket, on a shelf, under the couch—what have you. Make a note of their location so that you can pick up any leftovers.
3. Release the cat and watch the fun. If Felix is slow to catch on, place him near a treat and point him in its direction. Cats sight objects by movement, and may have trouble at first locating a stationary treat; he may pat it a couple of times to make sure it's food before eating it. Teach him to depend on his schnoz by using extra-smelly treats at first.

Waiting for Daddy

by Anonymouse

We are waiting for our daddy,
All washed, and dressed,
and nice.

We're glad, because,
We know he brings,
A basket-full
of mice.

So you've visited your local shelter, pet rescue organization, or breeder, met the perfect pet, and fallen in love. You've thought it over and are ready to welcome home your bouncing bundle of fur. Not so fast!

DON'T pick up your new charge without first setting up a good scratching post. The best ones are incorporated into a piece of multifunctional cat furniture. These allow the cat to scratch or climb to a platform or hammock that serves as a bed. Interwood Corporation and 4YourCat are two manufacturers of modular cat furniture. Or you can buy simple posts mounted on large, heavy bases that prevent wobbling. Look for stable posts taller than 30 inches and covered with sisal or jute, not carpeting. If your cat finds a really great scratching post waiting for him, there is no reason why he should choose your carpets over the post!

Arrival Day Checklist

DO find out what type of litter your new cat or kitten is accustomed to. We recommend using one with as few chemical additives as possible—especially with kittens. Set up a good-size litter tray in the room where he'll spend his first night.

DON'T plan on feeding your cat from your own dishes. Keep your china separate from your pet's (preferably stainless-steel) bowls. Pick up a stash of the food he has been eating; if you plan to make a dietary change, do it gradually.

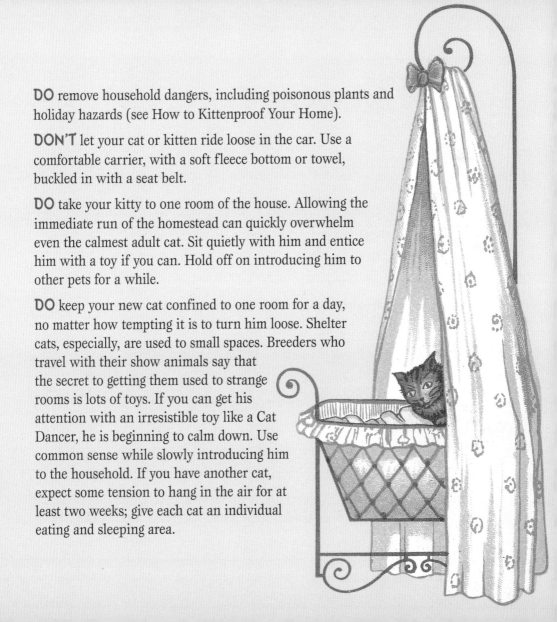

DO remove household dangers, including poisonous plants and holiday hazards (see How to Kittenproof Your Home).

DON'T let your cat or kitten ride loose in the car. Use a comfortable carrier, with a soft fleece bottom or towel, buckled in with a seat belt.

DO take your kitty to one room of the house. Allowing the immediate run of the homestead can quickly overwhelm even the calmest adult cat. Sit quietly with him and entice him with a toy if you can. Hold off on introducing him to other pets for a while.

DO keep your new cat confined to one room for a day, no matter how tempting it is to turn him loose. Shelter cats, especially, are used to small spaces. Breeders who travel with their show animals say that the secret to getting them used to strange rooms is lots of toys. If you can get his attention with an irresistible toy like a Cat Dancer, he is beginning to calm down. Use common sense while slowly introducing him to the household. If you have another cat, expect some tension to hang in the air for at least two weeks; give each cat an individual eating and sleeping area.

Beware of Kittens

by Heinrich Heine

Beware, my friend, of fiends and their grimaces;
   Of little angels' wiles yet more beware thee;
   Just such a one to kiss her did ensnare me,
But coming, I got wounds and not embraces.
Beware of black old cats, with evil faces;
   Yet more, of kittens white and soft be wary;
   My sweetheart was just such a little fairy,
And yet she well-nigh scratched my heart to pieces.
Oh child! oh sweet love, dear beyond all measure,
   How could those eyes, so bright and clear, deceive me?
   That little paw so sore a heart-wound give me?—
My kitten's tender paw, thou soft, small treasure—
   Oh! could I to my burning lips but press thee,
   My heart the while might bleed to death and bless thee.

58

La Chatte Saha

by Colette

No . . . it's you. It's you . . . you don't love me."

He backed up to the wall and pressed Camille against his hip. He could feel her shaking and cold from her shoulder to her knees, bare above the rolled stockings. She did not hold back; she yielded her whole body to him, faithfully.

"Ah, ah! I don't love you. So that's it! Another jealous scene on account of Saha?"

He could feel that whole body, pressed against his, stiffen—Camille recapturing her self-defense, her resistance; and he went on, encouraged by the moment and the opportunity.

"Instead of loving that charming animal the way I do. . . . Are we the only young married couple to bring up a cat or a dog? Would you like a parrot, a mar-moset, a pair of lovebirds to make me jealous?"

She shook her shoulders and protested by making a peevish sound in her closed mouth. His head high, Alain controlled his own voice and spurred himself on.

"Come now, come on. One or two more childish bickerings, and we'll get somewhere." She's like a jar I have to turn upside down in order to empty it completely. But come on. . . .

"Would you like a little lion, a baby crocodile, say, fifty years old or so? You'd do better to adopt Saha. If you'll just take the trouble, you'll see. . . ."

Camille wrenched herself from his arms so furiously that he tottered.

"No," she cried. "That? Never. You hear what I say? Never!"

She drew a long sigh of rage and repeated in a lower tone:

"No. . . . never!"

"That's that," he said to himself delightedly.

He pushed her into the bedroom, lowered the blinds, turned on the square ceiling lights, closed the window. With a quick movement Camille went to the window, which Alain reopened.

"On the condition that you don't scream," he said.

He rolled up the single armchair for Camille; he himself straddled the one small chair at the foot of the wide, turned-down, freshly sheeted bed. The glazed chintz curtains, drawn for the night, cast a shade of green over Camille's pallor and her crumpled white dress.

"So?" Alain began. "Impossible to settle? Horrible situation? Either she or you?"

An abrupt shake of the head was her answer and Alain was made to realize that he had better drop his bantering manner.

"What do you want me to tell you?" he began, after a silence. "The only thing I can't say? You know very well I won't give up that cat. I'd be ashamed to. Ashamed for my own sake, ashamed for her. . . ."

"I know," Camille said.

"And ashamed in your eyes," he finished.

He kept silent so long that she was angry again.

"Go on, say something. What are you waiting for?"

"The sequel," Alain said. "The end of the story."

He got up deliberately, bent over his wife, and lowered his voice as he indicated the French window.

"It was you, wasn't it? You pushed her off?"

She made a swift movement and put the bed between them, but she denied nothing.

With a kind of indulgent smile, he watched her flee.

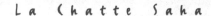

"You threw her," he said dreamily. "I felt that you had changed everything between us. You pushed her. She broke her claws trying to catch hold of the wall . . ."

He lowered his head, seeming to picture the crime. "But how did you throw her? By clutching her by the skin of her neck? By taking advantage of her sleeping on the balcony? Have you been planning the attack for a long time? Did you two quarrel beforehand?"

He raised his head, looked at Camille's hands and arms.

"No, you haven't any marks. It was she who accused you when I asked you to touch her. She was magnificent."

He turned from Camille to look at the night, the burnt-out stars, the tops of the three poplars with the bedroom lights shining upon them.

"Well," he said simply, "I'm leaving."

"Oh, listen . . . listen . . ."

Camille begged in a low voice.

But she did not hinder him from leaving the bedroom. He opened closet doors, talked to the cat in the bathroom, and from the sound of his footsteps Camille knew that he had just put on his street shoes. Mechanically she looked at the clock. He came back into the room, carrying Saha in a wide basket which Buque used when she went to market. Hastily dressed, his hair hardly combed, a handkerchief around his neck, he had the look of a lover after a quarrel. Wide eyed, Camille stared at him. But she heard Saha move in the basket and her lips tightened.

"There you are; I'm leaving," Alain said again.

He lowered his eyes, raised the basket slightly and, with designed cruelty, corrected himself:

"We're leaving."

There is no more intrepid explorer than a kitten.

—Jules Champfleury

Kittenproofing

The second you open a cupboard door, she's there. If you look away for an instant, she'll disappear, only to materialize underfoot. And just like a toddler, she puts everything in her mouth. Congratulations, you're having a kitten! Your rambunctious bundle of joy is a terror on four legs with very little sense. The following suggestions are helpful for both kitten and cat owners:

■ First, save your upholstery. Set up a wonderful scratching post before the kitten sets foot in your home. We cannot stress this enough. This way, your new addition will be trained to the post immediately, and not condition herself to use the love seat you inherited from your favorite aunt. Don't wait till after she comes home to run out to buy a post—that's too late, and you will end up with the difficult task of trying to teach a cat to stop scratching your furniture and carpets. Remember: Cats *must* scratch to groom their claws.

■ Go on "crevice patrol." Examine your baseboards and floors for holes, jagged edges, and nails. Don't allow a tiny kitten the opportunity to get in between the studs of a wall or the joists in a floor. Tape down or cover electrical cords to prevent chewing and electrical shocks.

■ Run your hand along the front baseplate of your cabinets and fill the holes. If your cabinets are on legs, is the space underneath clear enough for the kitten to get in and out easily? Can she climb up behind a unit and get stuck between it and the wall? You may have to block access to this space with heavy cardboard or wood until your kitten is larger and smarter.

■ Next, open the doors of all base cabinets and run your hand along the backs at the bottom. Is there a space at the floor between the cabinet and the wall that a kitten could fit into and, from there, jam herself under the base? Examine the interiors of wall cabinets, too, for any holes. Make sure your kitten can't climb through and end up behind a wall panel between upper and lower cabinets.

■ Block off fireplaces, attic, and other off-limits areas. Kittens won't hesitate to climb partway up the inside of a chimney and get covered with creosote; this requires an emergency vet visit and detergents. Remind family members that certain doors must always be kept shut (hang signs, if necessary). Put lids on toilet seats down; kittens are prone to falling in.

■ Place all household cleaners, tools, garbage, medicines, and sharp equipment in off-limits locations. Mothballs and phenols found in some disinfectants are toxic. Antifreeze actually attracts dogs and cats with its sweet flavor, and will kill them. Get rid of poisonous plants and holiday hazards.

■ Remove knickknacks from open surfaces. Don't leave items that a kitten could swallow lying around.

■ Examine commercial pet toys and remove any decorations that your pet could chew off and swallow.

■ Thread, fishing line, and dental floss are strictly off-limits for cats of any age. If swallowed, these can wrap themselves around a section of intestine and require emergency surgery to save your pet's life. Some cats have a compulsion to swallow wool yarn. Use string or twine for supervised playtime.

■ Finally, monitor a kitten carefully the first day you give her run of the house. Note her personality traits and unique brand of mischief. Keep her bed, litter box, post, food, and toys in an area that you can close off, like a den or bedroom, in case you have to leave her alone. Enjoy! Kittenhood is gone in a flash.

Kitty Poosball

Have a bored cat? Watch her come alive for this challenge. It's a little like foosball with paws. Cats peer through the top, figuring out how to get the toys out, while reaching in through the side holes to bat them around. It can busy them for hours if the holes are too small to get the objects out easily. While store-bought versions are available, we recommend making this model first.

rectangular, shallow cardboard boxes (like the type used for cat food cans or file folders); utility or X-Acto knife; small items such as Ping-Pong balls, catnip toys, sparkle balls, etc.; strapping tape

1. Use the top and bottom of an office-supply box or two cat-food-can cases to make a top that fits over a bottom. Cut two holes in each short end of the top box, just big enough to poke a Ping-Pong ball through. Cut three holes in each long edge. Cut three rows of two holes each in the top.

2. Place the top over the bottom and trace the holes on the sides of the bottom box; cut these out so that holes go all the way through. Load the box with five or six toys (Ping-Pong balls and small catnip toys are great) and close it. Tape the bottom and top together securely, reinforcing it with tape so it won't collapse if your cat jumps on top of it.

How Many?

So you've brought home a new cat or kitten and are wondering whether he must have a playmate in order not to be lonely. Behaviorists who have studied feral cat colonies for years still answer this question with a no. Dogs kept from other dogs usually have some issues, whereas cats do not require the companionship of their own species. Although small cats in groups learn to tolerate and even greet each other to keep the peace, they hunt alone, are not pack animals like dogs, and display competitive, not cooperative, behavior. Lion prides are the only cat groups that cooperate, and only because they hunt very large prey.

There is, of course, nothing wrong with having more than one cat; even house cats need their space, or territory, however, and will display jealousy to varying degrees—sometimes arguing over who gets to sleep closest to the human. And bathing each other can turn inexplicably into a spat, and then turn just as inexplicably into a communal nap. How many cats are too many? This varies with the household,and the disposition of the particular cats, but vets seem to agree that as a general rule of thumb, keeping four cats in a city apartment is getting close to the borderline.

Once upon a time, and long, long ago, a little boy was left in the care of a group of monks at a temple in the country-side. In a short time, the monks learned that there was one thing this boy loved to do above all else, and that was draw. His skill was extraordinary, and so to encourage him, the monks allowed him the free-dom to draw anything he liked. And the things he loved to draw above all else were cats.

The Boy Who Drew Cats

A Japanese Legend

Maybe they allowed him too much freedom, for as he got older, they realized that his drawing was growing out of control. Instead of restraining his artwork to parchment, his beautiful creations were sprawled across walls, etched into screens, and even displayed on the floor! Everywhere one turned, small cats peeked out from corners, large cats stretched beneath windows, cats with fierce eyes glared at meek cats gently cleaning themselves on rice paper screens. The monks began to complain.

"Our temple should be a place of simplicity and purity. How can one worship if everywhere we look, there are cats ready to spring at us?" one asked.

The eldest monk of the temple shook his head. "This will not do. The boy must learn some restraint." And so he called the boy to him.

"My boy, you have lived with us for many years. We have all seen your talent grow from a tiny seed into a beautiful flower." The boy blushed with pride and gently stroked a paintbrush he was holding, "But your paintings are disrupting the routine of our fellow monks."

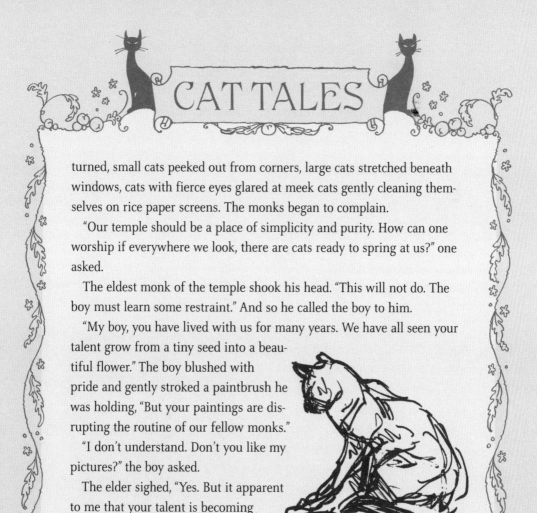

"I don't understand. Don't you like my pictures?" the boy asked.

The elder sighed, "Yes. But it apparent to me that your talent is becoming

chaotic. Perhaps you have been confined to this temple for too long. I feel that is best for you to travel out into the world. Maybe then you will find a way to focus your art."

The boy was sad to hear that the elder wanted him to leave, but at the same time, a tiny flame of excitement flickered within his heart. He had always wondered what lay beyond the grounds of the temple, and now he would finally get his chance to find out!

After saying his good-byes and packing his few belongings, including his precious paintbrushes and ink, the boy set off into the countryside. He walked for miles and miles, but hardly seemed tired. He had never been this far from the temple before and everything he saw seemed new and wonderful to him.

"I could stop and stay here for the rest of my life, and still not run out of things to paint," he declared as he took in the view from a gently rolling hill.

CAT TALES

But as eager as he was to see what lay just beyond the next rise, dusk soon began to fall, and the boy realized he needed to find shelter for the night. He had just made his way through a thick grove of trees, when suddenly he saw a large temple sitting atop a hill.

"The monks will gladly let me stay there for the night," he thought and made his way towards the large structure.

But as he got closer, he saw that the temple grounds were in great disrepair. After knocking at the door and getting no answer, the boy let himself into the temple, and discovered that it had not been used in some time.

"I wonder why that is," he murmured. But the mystery was pushed out of his head when he lit a lamp and saw that the walls of the temple were a beautiful, smooth white. It looked exactly like one giant canvas, and the boy gasped at the possibilities.

He quickly set up his paintbrush and ink, and began drawing on every square inch of available space. He painted coy cats with curlicue tails, and sweet cats with velvety eyes. He didn't stop until all of the walls had been covered by one hundred different felines in one hundred different poses. After such a grand undertaking, he was exhausted and eagerly made a bed

CAT TALES

CAT TALES

on the temple floor. But after lying down, he found that he could not sleep.

He tossed and turned, and turned and tossed, and finally gathered up his blankets.

"I don't know why it is, but this room makes me very uneasy," he thought, and after investigating the rest of the temple, he found a small closet to the side of the main room, The boy arranged his bed inside that and gently closed the door.

No sooner had his eyes shut, when a terrible snarl came from outside. Petrified with fear, the boy lay frozen in the dark as the horrible sound echoed again and again. Suddenly, he heard a loud thumping noise, accompanied by a chorus of howls and screams. It sounded as if a ferocious battle was taking place right outside the closet door, but the boy was too scared to even peek out! He listened to the gruesome noises for what seemed like hours, until, suddenly, after one final, agonizing scream, the room fell silent. The boy shook in his bed and waited desperately for the dawn to come.

When a tiny sliver of light finally slipped under the closet door, the boy gathered up his courage and slowly stepped out into the main room.

CAT TALES

There he discovered the lifeless body of a hideous rat, the size of a small horse, lying in the middle of the room!

Such a disgusting rat would have snapped him right in two if he had slept in the main room the night before, and the thought made him weak. But what had saved him from such a horrible fate and vanquished this terrible enemy? He looked around the room, and although he found signs of a battle, he could see no weapons of any kind.

The boy was about to gather his things and leave as fast his legs could carry him, when he noticed that one of his painted cats appeared to have a red circle around his mouth.

"But I have no red paint," the boy thought. He slowly examined his other paintings, and discovered that other cats seemed to have bits of fur stuck to the wall where their claws were drawn. In fact, now that he looked closely, all of the cats seemed to be in completely different positions than before!

"Could it be that my painted cats have saved me?" the boy wondered. Silently thanking his wonderful creations, he gathered his things and left the temple as fast as he could. After walking a short distance, he came to a village and explained what had happened at the first shop he came to.

"You mean you've killed the demon of the temple?" the shopkeeper exclaimed. He quickly spread the news, and the villagers gathered and told the boy that for as long as anyone could remember, a monstrous demon that took the shape of a giant rat had plagued the temple, making it impossible for the villagers to worship. When they realized their ancient enemy was now defeated, they cheered and carried the boy on their shoulders throughout the village, proclaiming him a hero.

The boy never discovered how his magical drawings had saved him that night, but he did believe that his art had rescued him from a terrible fate. As he grew older, the boy learned to draw other things, and he became a famous artist throughout the land. It was said that his pictures seemed so real, so lifelike, they might someday jump right off the canvas.

But none were more realistic than the hundred cats he drew that night in the temple, long, long ago.

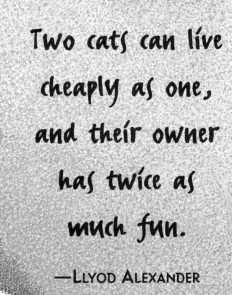

Two cats can live cheaply as one, and their owner has twice as much fun.

—LLYOD ALEXANDER

Clicker Training Step 2
The Touch

The final goal of the Touch is to get the cat to press her nose to the end of the prop. It's a basic building block for other training. During this first trick, both you and your cat will be learning. Very experienced trainers can teach a "green" cat a new behavior in a matter of minutes.

Clicker (see page 36), 20–30 treats, chopstick or plastic straw

1. Prepare to click immediately. Hold the stick about 2 or 3 inches from your cat's face. As—not *after*—he looks at it, click, and then treat. Don't wiggle the prop around. Don't touch him with it or make noises.
2. If she paws or bites the prop, don't click; withdraw it for a few seconds and slowly hold it out again. She will realize eventually that out-of-control pawing will not get her the treats she smells.
3. Click each time the cat makes the tiniest head motion toward the stick, and then treat. Don't ask for perfection. Treat, then repeat. He will soon figure out that he's "getting paid" for doing a very simple thing.
4. You may get lucky: Your cat may touch the prop with her nose right away. *CLICK!* Hit that clicker while it is happening,

and before kitty paws it or does something else you don't want, hand her two treats (reinforcements) to let her know "That's IT!"

5. After 20 or so treats, put the clicker, prop, and treats away till another session. Don't leave items out, or kitty can get the idea that they are toys.

6. It could take a couple of sessions per day over a week, each involving 20 treats, or it may happen sooner. Once your cat "gets it" (this is called *startling*) and is repeating the behavior, try presenting the prop slightly to one side and then the other. Click the instant his head follows. Try to increase the repetition speed, then the distance you hold the prop away. Back up and start over if he walks away, begins rubbing everything, or appears to forget.

7. Eventually begin adding the verbal cue, "Touch," just before the cat touches the prop.

Once you've gotten some fairly consistent results over several days, your cat will get excited the moment the prop and clicker come out. You now have a "clicker-wise" pet!

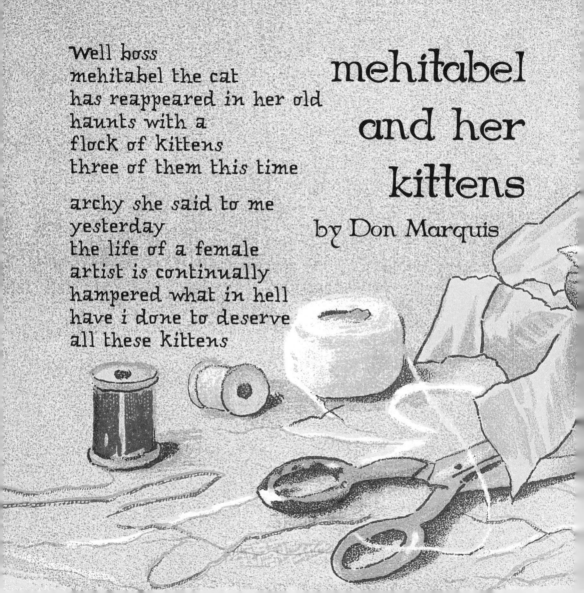

mehitabel and her kittens

by Don Marquis

Well boss
mehitabel the cat
has reappeared in her old
haunts with a
flock of kittens
three of them this time

archy she said to me
yesterday
the life of a female
artist is continually
hampered what in hell
have i done to deserve
all these kittens

CAT TALES

nce upon a time, a man was given a cat as a birthday present. The feline was a beautiful dark grey with bright, sparkling eyes and a patch of white at its throat.

"Such a handsome cat deserves a very fine name!" the man declared to the party guests, as he stroked its soft head.

"You should name him Tiger!" suggested one guest, "That way he will be as fierce as a tiger when it comes to fighting battles in the alley!"

"Nonsense," another interrupted. "You should name him Dragon. He will possess the strength of ten tigers, as well as a noble temperament to boot."

A third guest bent to scoop the cat up in her arms. "Why not name him Cloud? Clouds are strong enough for even dragons to lie on, and they are as graceful as a flock of butterflies."

"Pshaw," a portly guest added, "but what moves the clouds to its whim? Why, the wind, of course!" He reached over to pet the cat and continued, "Call this cat Wind and he

What's In a Name?

A Chinese Folktale

will be as wily and playful as the invisible breezes!"

"The winds are indeed crafty," another friend said as the cat leapt out of the lady's arms, "and there's only one thing that can stop them: a wall. A cat named Wall will be as steadfast as brick and as sure as granite."

"My friends," said one other guest, who perhaps had had a bit too much to drink, "all of these are wonderful suggestions. All walls are very diffi-cult to overcome. But," here he raised a swaying finger, "what is the one thing that can find its way through a wall as easily as water? Why, a mouse, of course! Call it Mouse!"

"Oh, for heaven's sake," the host bellowed, as the party broke out in laughter. "A cat will be grace-ful and strong, fierce and playful, steadfast and clever with any name. After all, a cat is a cat no matter what I call it. So why on earth should I name it anything else?"

And Cat seemed to think this was very wise indeed.

What's in a Name?

According to a study of veterinarians by the ASPCA, the top 10 pet names are:

Max

Sam

Lady

Bear

Smokey

Shadow

Kitty

Molly

Buddy

Brandy

The 20 top cat names, based on production of hundreds of thousands of pet ID tags, are:

Tigger	Lucky
Tiger	Misty
Max	Sammy
Smokey	Princess
Sam	Oreo
Kitty	Samantha
Sassy	Charlie
Shadow	Boots
Simba	Oliver
Patch	Lucy

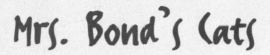

Mrs. Bond's Cats

by James Herriot

The lady and I established an immediate rapport which was strengthened by the fact that I was always prepared to spend time over her assorted charges; crawling on my stomach under piles of logs in the outhouse to reach the outside cats, coaxing them down from trees, stalking them endlessly through the shrubbery. But from my point of view it was rewarding in many ways.

For instance there was the diversity of names she had for her cats. True to her London upbringing she had named many of the Toms after the great Arsenal team of those days. There was Eddie Hapgood, Cliff Bastin, Ted Drake, Wilf Copping, but she did slip up in one case because Alex James had kittens three times a year with unfailing regularity.

Then there was her way of calling them home. The first time I saw her at this was on a still summer evening.

The two cats she wanted me to see were out in the garden somewhere and I walked with her to the back door where she halted, clasped her hands across her bosom, closed her eyes and gave tongue in a mellifluous contralto.

"Bates, Bates, Bates, Ba-hates." She actually sang out the words in a reverent monotone except for a delightful little lilt on the "Ba-hates." Then once more she inflated her ample rib cage like an operatic prima donna and out it came again, delivered with the utmost feeling.

"Bates, Bates, Bates, Ba-hates."

Anyway it worked, because Bates the cat came trotting from behind a clump of laurel. There remained the other patient and I watched Mrs. Bond with interest.

She took up the same stance, breathed in, closed her eyes, composed her features into a

sweet half-smile and started again.

"Seven-times-three, Seven-times-three, Seven-times-three-hee." It was set to the same melody as Bates with the same dulcet rise and fall at the end. She didn't get the quick response this time, though, and had to go through the performance again and again, and as the notes lingered on the still evening air the effect was startlingly like a muezzin calling the faithful to prayer.

At length she was successful and a fat tortoiseshell slunk apologetically along the wall-side into the house.

"By the way, Mrs. Bond," I asked, making my voice casual. "I didn't quite catch the name of that last cat."

"Oh, Seven-times-three?" She smiled reminiscently. "Yes, she is a dear. She's had three kittens seven times running, you see, so I thought it rather a good name for her, don't you?"

"Yes, yes, I do indeed. Splendid name, splendid."

The Naming of Cats

by T. S. Eliot

The Naming of Cats is a difficult matter,

    It isn't just one of your holiday games;

You may think at first I'm as mad as a hatter

When I tell you, a cat must have THREE DIFFERENT NAMES.

First of all, there's the name that the family use daily,

    Such as Peter, Augustus, Alonzo or James,

Such as Victor or Jonathan, George or Bill Bailey—

    All of them sensible everyday names.

There are fancier names if you think they sound sweet

    Some for the gentlemen, some for the dames:

Such as Plato, Admetus, Electra, Demeter—

    But all of them sensible everyday names.

But I tell you, a cat needs a name that's particular,

A name that's peculiar, and more dignified,
Else how can he keep up his tail perpendicular,
Or spread out his whiskers, or cherish his pride?
Of names of this kind, I can give you a quorum,
Such as Munkustrap, Quaxo, or Coricopat,
Such as Bombalurina, or else Jellylorum—
Names that never belong to more than one cat.
But above and beyond there's still one name left over,
And that is the name that you never will guess;
The name that no human research can discover—
But THE CAT HIMSELF KNOWS, and will never confess.
When you notice a cat in profound meditation,
The reason, I tell you, is always the same:
His mind is engaged in a rapt contemplation
Of the thought, of the thought, of the thought of his name:
His ineffable effable
Effanineffable
Deep and inscrutable singular Name.

Cheesy Treats

Especially for critters with a "cheese" tooth, these tasty wonders are made with all human-grade ingredients from your pantry. Every member of the family, feline and otherwise, can enjoy Cheesy Treats. So, don't be surprised if you find a hand in the cheesy jar!

1 cup flour
$1/2$ cup cornmeal
1 egg, beaten
$1/4$ cup water
$2/3$ cup grated Parmesan cheese, divided
sprinkling of salt

1. Preheat the oven to 300°F.
2. Combine all the ingredients except half the cheese. Flour your hands and knead until thoroughly mixed.
3. On a floured surface, roll the dough into long, thin "worms" with floured hands. Pull apart into 1-inch pieces.
4. Roll the pieces in the remaining cheese and place them on a greased baking sheet.
5. Bake for 10–12 minutes. Store in a sealed container in the fridge for up to 2 weeks. These can be broken apart into cheesy kibble-size treats.

Makes about 4 cups.

Cat Resolutions

I will not flush the toilet while my human is in the shower. ■ I will not use the humans' bathtub to store live mice for late-night snacks. ■ I will not eat large numbers of assorted bugs, then come home and barf them up so the humans can see that I'm getting plenty of roughage. ■ I will not perch on my human's chest in the middle of the night and stare into her eyes until she wakes up. ■ As fast as I am, I must remember that I cannot run through closed doors. ■ I will remember that I am a walking static generator. My human does not need my help

Feline Funnies

installing a new board in her computer. ■ I will remember that my human really will wake up and feed me. I do not have to pry his eyelids open with my claws. ■ When my young humans are playing with modeling clay, I will not remove solid waste from my litter tray and roll it onto the kitchen floor. ■ I will not display my worm collection on the kitchen floor on a rainy night. My human does not like finding it with her bare feet. ■ I will not hide behind the toilet so that I can pat my human on the backside when he sits down just to make him levitate.

Calvin

by Charles Dudley Warner

Calvin is dead. His life, long to him, but short for the rest of us, was not marked by startling adventures, but his character was so uncommon and his qualities were so worthy of imitation, that I have been asked by those who personally knew him to set down my recollections of his career.

His origin and ancestry were shrouded in mystery; even his age was a matter of pure conjecture. Although he was of the Maltese race, I have reason to suppose that he was American by birth as he certainly was in sympathy. Calvin was given to me eight years ago by Mrs. Stowe, but she knew nothing of his age or origin. He walked into her house one day out of the great unknown and became at once at home, as if he had been always a friend of the family. He appeared to have artistic and literary tastes, and it was as if he had inquired at the door if that was the residence of the author of *Uncle Tom's Cabin*, and, upon being assured that it was, had decided to dwell there. This is, of course, fanciful, for his antecedents were wholly unknown, but in his time he could hardly have been in any household where he would not have heard *Uncle Tom's Cabin* talked about. When he came to Mrs. Stowe, he was as large as he ever was, and apparently as old as he ever became. Yet there was in him no appearance of age; he was in the happy maturity of all his powers, and you would rather have said that in that maturity he had found the secret of perpetual youth. And it was as difficult to believe that he would ever be aged as it was to imagine that he had ever been in immature youth. There was in him a mysterious perpetuity.

After some years, when Mrs. Stowe made her winter home in Florida, Calvin came to live with us. From the first moment, he fell into the ways of the house and assumed a recognized position in the family,—I say recognized, because after he became known he was always inquired for by visitors, and in the letters to the other members of the family he always received a message. Although the least obtrusive of beings, his individuality always made itself felt.

His personal appearance had much to do with this, for he was of royal mold, and had an air of high breeding. He was large, but he had nothing of the fat grossness of the celebrated Angora family; though powerful, he was exquisitely proportioned, and as graceful in every movement as a young leopard. When he stood up to open a door—he opened all the doors with old-fashioned latches—he was portentously tall, and when stretched on the rug before the fire he seemed too long for this world— as indeed he was. His coat was the finest and softest I have ever seen, a shade of quiet Maltese; and from his throat downward, underneath, to the white tips of his feet, he wore the whitest and most delicate ermine; and no person was ever more fastidiously neat. In his finely formed head you saw something of his aristocratic character; the ears were small and cleanly cut, there was a tinge of pink in the nostrils, his face was handsome, and the expression of his countenance exceedingly intelligent—I should call it even a sweet expression if the term were not inconsistent with his look of alertness and sagacity.

Calvin

It is difficult to convey a just idea of his gayety in connection with his dignity and gravity, which his name expressed. As we know nothing of his family, of course it will be understood that Calvin was his Christian name. He had times of relaxation into utter playfulness, delighting in a ball of yarn, catching sportively at stray ribbons when his mistress was at her toilet, and pursuing his own tail, with hilarity, for lack of anything better. He could amuse himself by the hour, and he did not care for children; perhaps something in his past was present to his memory. He had absolutely no bad habits, and his disposition was perfect. I never saw him exactly angry, though I have seen his tail grow to an enormous size when a strange cat appeared upon his lawn. He disliked cats, evidently regarding them as feline and treacherous, and he had no association with them. Occasionally there would be heard a night concert in the shrubbery. Calvin would ask to have the door opened, and then you would hear a rush and a "pestzt," and the concert would explode, and Calvin would quietly come in and resume his seat on the hearth. There was no trace of anger in his manner, but he wouldn't have any of that about the house. He had the rare virtue of magnanimity.

Although he had fixed notions about his own rights, and extraordinary persistency in getting them, he never showed temper at a repulse; he simply and firmly persisted till he had what he wanted. His diet was one point; his idea was that of the scholars about

105

dictionaries—to "get the best." He knew as well as anyone what was in the house, and would refuse beef if turkey was to be had; and if there were oysters, he would wait over the turkey to see if the oysters would not be forthcoming. And yet he was not a gross gourmand; he would eat bread if he saw me eating it, and thought he was not being imposed on. His habits of feeding, also, were refined; he never used a knife, and he would put up his hand and draw the fork down to his mouth as grace-fully as a grown person. Unless necessity compelled, he would not eat in the kitchen, but insisted upon his meals in the dining-room, and would wait patiently, unless a stranger were present; and then he was sure to importune the visitor, hoping that the latter was ignorant of the rule of the house, and would give him something. They used to say that he pre-ferred as his tablecloth on the floor a certain well-known church journal;

but this was said by an Episcopalian. So far as I know, he had no religious prejudices, except that he did not like the association with Romanists. He tolerated the servants, because they belonged to the house, and would sometimes linger by the kitchen stove; but the moment visitors came in he arose, opened the door, and marched into the drawing-room. Yet he enjoyed the company of his equals, and never withdrew, no matter how many callers—whom he recognized as of his society—might come into the drawing-room. Calvin was fond of company, but he wanted to choose it; and I have no doubt that his was an aristocratic fastidiousness rather than one of faith. It is so with most people.

The intelligence of Calvin was something phenomenal, in his rank of life. He established a method of communicating his wants, and even some of his sentiments; and he could help himself in many things. There was a furnace register in a retired room, where he used to go when he wished to be alone, that he always opened when he desired more heat; but never shut it, any more than he shut the door after himself. He could do almost everything but speak; and you would declare sometimes that you could see a pathetic longing to do that in his intelligent face. I have no desire to overdraw his qualities, but if there was one thing in him more noticeable than another, it was his fondness for nature. He could content himself for hours at a low window, looking into the ravine and at the great trees, noting the smallest stir there; he delighted, above all things, to accompany me walking about the garden, hearing the birds, getting the smell of the fresh earth, and rejoicing in the sunshine. He followed me and gamboled like a dog, rolling over on the turf and exhibiting his delight in a hundred ways. If I worked, he sat and watched me, or looked off over the bank, and kept his ear open to the twitter in the cherry trees. When it stormed, he was sure to sit at the window, keenly watching the rain or the snow, glancing up and down at its falling; and a winter tempest always delighted him. I think he was genuinely fond of birds, but, so far as I know, he usually confined himself to one a day; he never killed, as some sportsmen do, for the sake of killing, but only as civilized people do—from necessity. He was intimate with the flying squirrels who dwell in the chestnut trees—too intimate, for almost every day in the summer he would bring in one, until he nearly discouraged them. He was, indeed, a superb hunter, and would have been a devastating one, if his bump of destructiveness had not been offset by a bump of moderation. There was very little of the brutality of the lower animals about him; I don't think he enjoyed rats for themselves, but he knew his business, and for the first few months of his residence with us he waged an awful campaign against the horde, and after that his simple presence was sufficient to deter them from coming on the premises. Mice amused him, but he usually considered them too small game to be taken seriously; I have seen him play for an hour with a mouse, and then let him go with a royal condescension. In this whole matter of "getting a living," Calvin was a great contrast to the rapacity of the age in which he lived.

I hesitate a little to speak of his capacity for friendship and the affectionateness of his nature, for I know from his own reserve that he would not care to have it much talked about. We understood each other perfectly,

but we never made any fuss about it; when I spoke his name and snapped my fingers, he came to me; when I returned home at night, he was pretty sure to be waiting for me near the gate, and would rise and saunter along the walk, as if his being there were purely accidental,—so shy was he commonly of showing feeling; and when I opened the door he never rushed in, like a cat, but loitered, and lounged, as if he had had no intention of going in, but would con-descend to. And yet, the fact was, he knew din-ner was ready, and he was bound to be there. He kept the run of dinner-time. It happened sometimes, during our absence in the summer, that dinner would be early, and Calvin, walking about the grounds, missed it and came in late. But he never made a mistake the second day. There was one thing he never did,—he never rushed through an open doorway. He never forgot his dig-nity. If he had asked to have the door opened, and was eager to go out, he always went deliberately; I can see him now, standing on the sill, looking about at the sky as if he was thinking whether it were worth while to take an umbrella, until he was near having his tail shut in.

His friendship was rather constant than demonstra-tive. When we returned from an absence of nearly two years, Calvin welcomed us with evident pleasure, but showed his satisfaction rather by tranquil happiness than by fuming about. He had the faculty of making us glad to get home. It was his constancy that was so attractive. He liked companionship, but he wouldn't be petted, or fussed over, or sit in any one's lap a moment; he always extricated himself from such familiarity with dignity and with no show of temper. If there was any petting to be done, however, he chose to do it. Often he would sit looking at me, and then, moved by a delicate affection, come and pull at my coat and sleeve until he could touch my face with his nose, and then go away contented. He had a habit of coming to my study in the morning, sitting quietly by my side or on the table for hours, watching the pen run over the paper, occasionally swinging his tail round for a blotter, and then going to sleep among the papers by the inkstand. Or, more rarely, he would watch the writing from a perch on my shoulder. Writing always interested him, and, until he understood it, he wanted to hold the pen.

He always held himself in a kind of reserve with his friend, as if he had said, "Let us respect our personality, and not make a 'mess' of friendship." He saw, with Emerson, the risk of degrading it to trivial conveniency. "Why insist on rash personal relations with your friend?" "Leave this touching and clawing." Yet I would not give an unfair notion of his aloofness, his fine sense of the sacredness of the me and the not-me. And, at the risk of not being believed, I will relate an incident, which was often repeated. Calvin had the practice of passing a portion of the night in the contemplation of its beauties, and would come into our chamber over the roof of the conservatory through the open window, summer and winter, and go to sleep on the foot of my bed. He would do this always exactly in this way; he never was content to stay in the chamber if we compelled him to go upstairs and through the door. He had the obstinacy of General Grant. But this is by the way. In the morning, he performed his toilet and went down to breakfast with the rest of the family. Now, when the mistress was absent from home, and at no other time, Calvin would come in the morning, when the bell rang, to the head of the bed, put up his feet and look into my face, follow me about when I rose, "assist" at the dressing, and in many purring ways show his fondness, as if he had plainly said, "I know that she has gone away, but I am here." Such was Calvin in rare moments.

He had his limitations. Whatever passion he had for nature, he had no conception of art. There was sent to him once a fine and very expressive cat's head in bronze, by Frémiet. I placed it on the floor. He regarded it intently, approached it cautiously and crouchingly, touched it with his nose, perceived the fraud, turned away abruptly, and never would notice it afterward. On the whole, his life was not only a successful one, but a happy one. He never had but one fear, so far as I know: he had a mortal and a reasonable terror of plumbers. He would never stay in the house when they were here. No coaxing could quiet him. Of course he didn't share our fear about their charges, but he must have had some dreadful experience with them in that portion of his life which is unknown to us. A plumber was to him the devil, and I have no doubt that, in his scheme, plumbers were foreordained to do him mischief.

Calvin

In speaking of his worth, it has never occurred to me to estimate Calvin by the worldly standard. I know that it is customary now, when anyone dies, to ask how much he was worth, and that no obituary in the newspapers is considered complete without such an estimate. The plumbers in our house were one day overheard to say that, "They say that *she* says that *he* says that he wouldn't take a hundred dollars for him." It is unnecessary to say that I never made such a remark, and that, so far as Calvin was concerned, there was no purchase in money.

As I look back upon it, Calvin's life seems to me a fortunate one, for it was natural and unforced. He ate when he was hungry, slept when he was sleepy, and enjoyed existence to the very tips of his toes and the end of his expressive and slow-moving tail. He delighted to roam about the garden, and stroll among the trees, and to lie on the green grass and

luxuriate in all the sweet influences of summer. You could never accuse him of idleness, and yet he knew the secret of repose. The poet who wrote so prettily of him that his little life was rounded with a sleep, understated his felicity; it was rounded with a good many. His conscience never seemed to interfere with his slumbers. In fact, he had good habits and a contented mind. I can see him now walk in at the study door, sit down by my chair, bring his tail artistically about his feet, and look up at me with unspeakable happiness in his handsome face. I often thought that he felt the dumb limitation which denied him the power of language. But since he was denied speech, he scorned the inarticulate mouthings of the lower animals. The vulgar mewing and yowling of the cat species was beneath him; he sometimes uttered a sort of articulate and well-bred ejaculation, when he wished to call attention to something that he considered remarkable, or to some want of his, but he never went whining about. He would sit for hours at a closed window, when he desired to enter, without a murmur, and when it was opened he never admitted that he had been impatient by "bolting" in. Though speech he had not, and the unpleasant kind of utterance given to his race he would not use, he had a mighty power of purr to express his measureless content with congenial society. There was in him a musical organ with stops of varied power and expression, upon which I have no doubt he could have performed Scarlatti's celebrated cat's-fugue.

Whether Calvin died of old age, or was carried off by one of the diseases incident to youth, it is impossible to say; for his departure was as quiet as his advent was mysterious. I only know that he appeared to us

Calvin

in this world in his perfect stature and beauty, and that after a time, like Lohengrin, he withdrew. In his illness there was nothing more to be regretted than in all his blameless life. I suppose there never was an illness that had more of dignity and sweetness and resignation in it. It came on gradually, in a kind of listlessness and want of appetite. An alarming symptom was his preference for the warmth of a furnace-register to the lively sparkle of the open wood-fire. Whatever pain he suffered, he bore it in silence, and seemed only anxious not to obtrude his malady. We tempted him with the delicacies of the season, but it soon became impossible for him to eat, and for two weeks he ate or drank scarcely anything. Sometimes he made an effort to take something, but it was evident that he made the effort to please us. The neighbors—and I am convinced that the advice of neighbors is never good for anything—suggested catnip. He wouldn't even smell it. We had the attendance of an amateur practitioner of medicine, whose real office was the cure of souls, but nothing touched his case. He took what was offered, but it was with the air of one to whom the time for pellets was past. He sat or lay day after day almost motionless, never once making a display of those vulgar convulsions or contortions of pain which are so disagreeable to society. His favorite place was on the brightest spot of a Smyrna rug by the conservatory, where the sunlight fell and he could hear the fountain play. If we went to him and exhibited our interest in his condition, he always purred in recognition of our

Calvin

sympathy. And when I spoke his name, he looked up with an expression that said, "I understand it, old fellow, but it's no use." He was to all who came to visit him a model of calmness and patience in affliction.

I was absent from home at the last, but heard by daily postal-card of his failing condition; and never again saw him alive. One sunny morning, he rose from his rug, went into the conservatory (he was very thin then), walked around it deliberately, looking at all the plants he knew, and then went to the bay-window in the dining-room, and stood a long time looking out upon the little field, now brown and sere, and toward the garden, where perhaps the happiest hours of his life had been spent. It was a last look. He turned and walked away, laid himself down upon the bright spot in the rug, and quietly died.

It is not too much to say that a little shock went through the neighborhood when it was known that Calvin was dead, so marked was his individuality; and his friends, one after another, came in to see him. There was no sentimental nonsense about his obsequies; it was felt that any parade would have been distasteful to him. John, who acted as undertaker, prepared a candle-box for him, and I believe assumed a professional decorum; but there may have been the usual levity underneath, for I heard that he remarked in the kitchen that it was the "dryest wake he ever attended." Everybody, however, felt a fondness for Calvin, and regarded him with a certain respect. Between him and Bertha there existed a great friendship, and she apprehended his nature; she used to say that sometimes she was afraid of him, he looked at her so intelligently; she was never certain that he was what he appeared to be.

When I returned, they had laid Calvin on a table in an upper chamber by an open window. It was February. He reposed in a candle-box, lined about the edge with evergreen, and at his head stood a little wine-glass with flowers. He lay with his head tucked down in his arms—a favorite position of his before the fire—as if asleep in the comfort of his soft and exquisite fur. It was the involuntary exclamation of those who saw him, "How natural he looks!" As for myself, I said nothing. John buried him under the twin hawthorn-trees—one white and the other pink—in a spot where Calvin was fond of lying and listening to the hum of summer insects and the twitter of birds.

Perhaps I have failed to make appear the individuality of character that was so evident to those who knew him. At any rate, I have set down nothing concerning him but the literal truth. He was always a mystery. I did not know whence he came; I do not know whither he has gone. I would not weave one spray of falsehood in the wreath I lay upon his grave.

Catspeak

There are several *tell-tail* signs that your cat is making a statement and that you should be listening! Pay close attention to the tail, ears, and posture. Your cat's body language will reveal plenty about your cat's mood.

Dogs come when they are called;
cats take a message and get
back to you later.
—MARY BLY

TAII

Relaxed, low-riding tail: This sign means the cat is content and comfortable, and at ease with her surroundings. A cat with her tail held like this is usually relaxed and looking for entertainment.

Twitching tail: When the tail thumps or thrashes about, your cat is making it known that he is not a happy camper. What did you do this time?

Tall tail: A tail sticking straight up in the air as your cat approaches means she is feeling playful and affectionate.

EAR

Face Forward: Ears that face frontward seem to mean a cat is untroubled and serene.

Flat Ears: If the cat's ears are flattened against its face, this is a defensive gesture. This will often be accompanied by fluffed fur, which can indicate a scaredy-cat.

Flicking Ear: Cats naturally turn their ears in the direction of an intriguing sound.

POSTURE

Crouching Tiger: Cats crouch before they pounce.

Stiff Neck: A cat who holds its body stiff and straight is angry or disgruntled.

Belly Up: A cat who exposes its belly is very comfortable and feeling safe.

The animal kingdom came
faultily:
too wide in the rump or too
sad-headed.
Little by little they disposed
their proportions,
invented their landscape,
collected their graces and satellites,
    and took to the air.
Only the cat
issued
wholly a cat,
intact and vainglorious:
he came forth a consummate identity,
knew what he wanted, and walked tall.

Cat

by
Pablo
Neruda

Catnip Sock

You've seen them in the stores: dozens of catnip toys, catnip mice, even stuffed catnip vegetables. Don't be fooled by all the decorations and high prices. This old standby, the shapeless, lowly, homemade catnip sock may win first place in Most Mutilated Toy category. Cats love to sink teeth and claws into the soft, plush cotton knit. Don't be surprised if your furry friend carries it off to his "secret place."

Child's crew sock, scissors, needle and thread, elastic hair band, tissue paper, catnip

1. Depending on the size of the sock, cut the toe or foot section off and discard the cuff; otherwise, the toy will be too big.
2. Turn the toe section wrongside out. Place the elastic around the top edge. Fold over the edge to cover the band, as with a drawstring waistband, and stitch the edge securely. The casing makes a sturdier toy, and will prevent a rambunctious puss from pulling the elastic band off.
3. Snip a small rectangular notch out of the top edge. This will serve as a small opening for access to the elastic. Stitch around the edges of the notch so they don't fray. Turn the sock-bag right-side out and stuff with tissue paper and catnip.
4. Pull the elastic through the notch and loop it tightly around the top several times, like a rubber band around a ponytail, until it is very tight. Toss!
5. Replenish catnip as needed.

CAT TALES

There was once a merchant who, crossing the vast desert, stopped at an oasis to refresh himself. As he came to the still water, he discovered two robbers that were beating and robbing a man. The merchant immediately entered the fray, and managed to fight off the attackers, sending them running across the burning sands. He examined the barely conscious man, tended to his injuries, provided him with food, and shared his fire with him that night.

After the wounded man had recovered enough to be able to sit up and speak, he sat beside the merchant. The campfire glowed beneath the black skies, and for a while, neither man spoke. The fire flickered and danced, sending shadows across the smooth sands. Finally, the wounded man began, "Thank you for helping me. Those robbers came upon me by surprise as I was resting."

A Cat Made of Magic

A Tale from Ancient Persia

CAT TALES

The merchant shrugged. "It was nothing. I would only like someone to act the same if I were in your place."

"But few would," the stranger insisted. "Although I am not a rich man, I would like to reward you in my own way. This may seem like an odd question, but what it is that you most wish for?"

The merchant was silent as he considered the question. He gazed deep into the beautiful skies at the pinpricks of starlight. He followed the gray smoke from the campfire as it swirled and shaped itself into odd forms. He watched the fire itself as it played on the sand.

"I have a wonderful family waiting for me at home. I am in relatively good health. There is nothing I could want more in this world than to forever experience this moment, with the skies, the fire, and the desert," he finally said.

"Very well, I will grant your wish," said the stranger.

What the merchant didn't know was that the stranger was actually a powerful magician.

CAT TALES

With a low chant, he deftly gathered the smoke from the fire into a ball which he cupped in one hand. He reached up and smoothly plucked two stars from the ebony sky. He pulled a bit of flame from the campfire, and finally, he gathered a pinch of sand into his closed fist.

"Amazing," the merchant whispered.

The merchant couldn't quite tell what the magician did next, but it seemed as if he was molding something with these extraordinary objects, as one would with clay. After several moments of breathless anticipation, a faint sound drifted across the sand.

Out of the magician's powerful hands slipped a beautiful long-haired cat with fur the color of smoke, eyes as bright as stars that danced with a hidden flame, and (when she dainty licked the merchant's hand), a tongue as gritty as the sands of the desert!

The magician handed him the creature and said, "This cat is the perfect embodiment of all that you treasure at this moment. Take good care of her and you will never lose the memory." The merchant thanked the magician and took the magical cat home. And so, the Persian cat was created in this world.

Among animals, cats are
the top-hatted, frock-coated
statesmen going about their
affairs at their own pace.

—ROBERT STEARNS

A Breed Apart

Although less than 1 percent of the cats in the world are actually pedigreed cats, or purebreds with a specific family tree or ancestry, the ones that qualify often have a rich history and a number of distinguishing characteristics. Here are some interesting tidbits on some popular cat breeds:

ABYSSINIAN lore holds numerous theories—for instance, that they were brought to England from Ethiopia, or that they are a cross of preexisting tabbies and British "bunny" ticked cats. However, genetic studies show the likely origin as the Indian Ocean coast or Southeast Asia.

The **AMERICAN SHORTHAIR** was brought to the United States from England with the early Puritan settlers because of its rat-catching skills. Soon thereafter, however, its loving personality came to be valued as much as its ability to catch mice and other little creatures.

The **BIRMAN** cats were supposedly sacred companions to the Burman Kittah priests.

BURMESE cats are known for their friendly

and affectionate personalities, which are often compared to dogs'. They often cozy up to their owners and even learn to retrieve!

The **CHARTREUX**, or "French blue," is believed to have been raised as a companion for the French Carthusian monks. The name of the cat, however, arguably derives from a type of Spanish wool, also called chartreux, that was popular in the early 18th century.

First cousin to the Siamese, the **COLORPOINT SHORTHAIR** was developed essentially as a Siamese cat with a red gene. As the colorpoint has gained in popularity, breeders have introduced other colors, such as blue, lilac, and chocolate, into the color stream.

Affectionately referred to as the "lazy man's Persian," the **EXOTIC** has the same plush coat, but without all the grooming requirements. Best kept indoors, these cats are sweet, quiet, and extremely affectionate.

Ceramic images of the **JAPANESE BOBTAIL**, called *maneki-neko*, or the "beckoning cat," are traditional symbols of good luck.

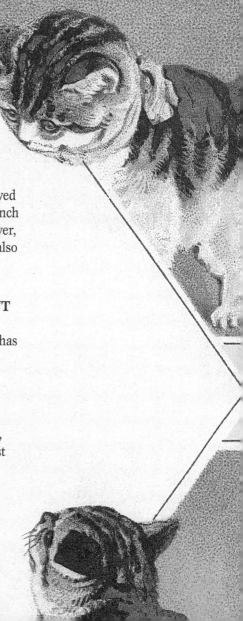

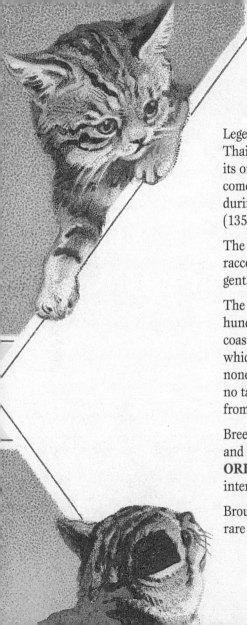

Legend has it that the **KORAT** was named by the Thai king Rama V after he learned the province of its origin. The earliest known picture of the Korat comes from *The Cat Book of Poems*, written during the Ayudhya Period of Siamese History (1350–1767).

The **MAINE COON** was once thought to be part raccoon, due to the fact that it is not only intelligent, but large and shaggy in appearance as well.

The **MANX** is believed to have originated hundreds of years ago on the Isle of Man off the coast of England. It is marked by its "missing tail," which has been attributed to a number of legends, none of which are true. In reality, the Manx has no tail because it comes from a different strain from other breeds of cats.

Breeders who wished to explore different color and pattern combinations developed the **ORIENTAL**. They are known for their intense interest in everyday human activities.

Brought from Persia to India in baskets alongside rare spices and jewels, **PERSIAN** cats are known for their long flowing coats, sweet pansylike faces, and remarkably melodious voices.

The **NORWEGIAN FOREST CAT** explored the world with the Vikings, protecting grain stores on land and sea.

The striking silver **RUSSIAN BLUE** was brought to England from an island in Northern Russia in the 1860s, where it is rumored to have become a favored pet of Queen Victoria.

A unique cat, the **SCOTTISH FOLD** acquired its name from the unusual manner in which its ears are folded against its head. While Scottish folds may produce offspring with either folded or normal ears, the folded-eared kittens are especially prized for their unique puppylike look.

The first **SIAMESE** to appear in England were a gift from Siam—now Thailand—to an English ambassador.

The **TONKINESE** originated from a breeding of a Siamese and a Burmese, and is credited with a wonderful memory as well as senses akin to radar.

How many cats does it take to screw in a lightbulb?

PERSIAN: "Lightbulb? What lightbulb?"

SOMALI: "The sun is shining, the day is young, we've got our whole lives ahead of us, and you're worrying about a burned-out lightbulb?"

NORWEGIAN FOREST CAT: "Just one. And I'll replace any wiring that's not up to date, too."

CORNISH REX: "Hey, guys, I've found the switch."

SPHYNX: "Turn it back on again, I'm cold."

EXOTIC: "Let the AOV do it. You can feed me while he's busy." (AOV: Any Other Variety.)

MANX: "Why change it? I can still pee on the carpet in the dark."

Feline Funnies

SIAMESE: "Make me!"

TURKISH ANGORA: "You need light to see?"

SINGAPURA: "I'll just blow in the AOV's ear and he'll do it."

BIRMAN: "Puh-leeez, dahling. I have servants for that kind of thing."

MAINE COON: "Oh, me, me! Pleeeeeeaze let me change the light-bulb! Can I, huh? Can I? Huh? Huh? Can I?"

RUSSIAN BLUE: "While it's dark, I'm going to sleep on the couch."

KORAT: "Korats are not afraid of the dark."

BRITISH SHORTHAIR: "Lightbulb? Lightbulb? That thing I ate was a lightbulb?"

BRITISH MOGGY: "None, catnap time is too precious to waste!"

Draggin' Dragon

The Cat Dancer (which makes a soft whirring sound), the beaded mouse (which rattles), and the Crinkle Sack, three of the most popular commercial cat toys around, owe their success in part to cats' love of all things rustly. This activity does, too. Most cats find chasing the dragon "irresistible," yet there are a few who react with the equivalent of "We are not amused." If your cat is at first afraid of it, lay it on the floor and let her sniff it over.

4–5 yards crinkly brown paper (like brown packaging paper but lighter in weight, yet heavier than ordinary tissue paper; find it at a packing or art supply store), scissors

1. Clear some space (say, a 30-foot run) so you won't be crashing into the furniture.

2. Crush the crinkly paper together lengthwise. Tie one knot in the middle and one knot about a foot from each end of the Dragon.

3. At one end, use the scissors to cut a fringe for the tail.

4. Grab the knot at the other end, or tie that end around your child's waist. Walk quickly with the Dragon trailing out behind you. Most cats love attacking the end, and even being gently dragged across the carpet.

Stately, kindly, lordly friend,
   Condescend
Here to sit by me, and turn
Glorious eyes that smile and burn,
Golden eyes, love's lustrous meed,
On the golden page I read.

All your wondrous wealth of hair,
   Dark and fair,
Silken-shaggy, soft and bright
As the clouds and beams of night,
Pays my reverent hand's caress
Back with friendlier gentleness.

Dogs may fawn on all and some,
   As they come;
You, a friend of loftier mind,
Answer friends alone in kind;
Just your foot upon my hand
Softly bids it understand.

Wild on woodland ways, your sires
   Flashed like fires;
Fair as flame, and fierce, and fleet,

To a Cat

by
Algernon
Charles
Swinburne

As with wings on wingless feet,
Shone and sprang your mother, free,
Bright and brave as wind or sea.

Free, and proud, and glad as they,
    Here to-day
Rests or roams their radiant child,
Vanquished not, but reconciled;
Free from curb of aught above
Save the lovely curb of love.

Love, through dreams of souls divine,
    Fain would shine
Round a dawn whose light and song
Then should right our mutual wrong,—
Speak, and seal the love-lit law,
Sweet Assisi's seer foresaw.

Dreams were theirs; yet haply may
    Dawn a day
When such friends and fellows born,
Seeing our earth as fair at morn,
May, for wiser love's sake, see
More of heaven's deep heart than we.

I have added a romantic inmate to
my family,—a large bloodhound, allowed to be the
finest dog of the kind in Scotland, perfectly gentle,
affectionate, good-natured, and the darling of all the
children. He is between the deer-greyhound and mastiff,
with a shaggy mane like a lion, and always sits beside me
at dinner, his head as high as the back of my
chair; yet it will gratify you to know that a
favorite cat keeps him in the greatest possible
order, insists upon all rights of precedence, and
scratches with impunity the nose of an animal who would
make no bones of a wolf, and pulls down a red deer without
fear or difficulty. I heard my friend set up some most
piteous howls (and I assure you the noise was no joke),
all occasioned by his fear of passing Puss, who had
stationed himself on the stairs.

—SIR WALTER SCOTT,
HINSE OF HINSEFELD

The Cat That Walked by Himself

by Rudyard Kipling

Hear and attend and listen; for this befell and behappened and became and was, O my Best Beloved, when the Tame animals were wild. The Dog was wild, and the Horse was wild, and the Cow was wild, and the Sheep was wild, and the Pig was wild–as wild as wild could be–and they walked in the Wet Wild Woods by their wild lones. But the wildest of all the wild animals was the Cat. He walked by himself, and all places were alike to him.

Of course the Man was wild too. He was dreadfully wild. He didn't even begin to be tame till he met the Woman, and she told him that she did not like living in his wild ways. She picked out a nice dry Cave, instead of a heap of wet leaves, to lie down in; and she strewed clean sand on the floor; and she lit a nice fire of wood at the back of the Cave; and she hung a dried wild-horse skin, tail-down, across the opening of the Cave; and she said, "Wipe your feet, dear, when you come in, and now we'll keep house."

That night, Best Beloved, they ate wild sheep roasted on the hot stones, and flavored with wild garlic and wild pepper; and wild duck stuffed with wild rice and wild fenugreek and wild coriander; and marrow-bones of wild oxen; and wild cherries, and wild grenadillas. Then the Man went to sleep in front of the fire ever so happy; but the Woman sat up, combing her hair. She took the bone of the shoulder of

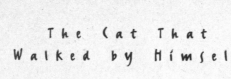

mutton—the big fat blade-bone—and she looked at the wonderful marks on it, and she threw more wood on the fire, and she made a Magic. She made the First Singing Magic in the world.

Out in the Wet Wild Woods all the wild animals gathered together where they could see the light of the fire a long way off, and they wondered what it meant.

Then Wild Horse stamped with his wild foot and said, "O my Friends and O my Enemies, why have the Man and the Woman made that great light in that great Cave, and what harm will it do us?"

Wild Dog lifted up his wild nose and smelled the smell of roast mutton, and said, "I will go up and see and look, and say; for I think it is good. Cat, come with me."

"Nenni!" said the Cat. "I am the Cat who walks by himself, and all places are alike to me. I will not come."

"Then we can never be friends again," said Wild Dog, and he trotted off to the Cave. But when he had gone a little way the Cat said to himself, "All places are alike to me. Why should I not go too and see and look and come away at my own liking." So he slipped after Wild Dog softly, very softly, and hid himself where he could hear everything.

When Wild Dog reached the mouth of the Cave he lifted up the dried horse-skin with his nose and sniffed the beautiful smell of the roast mutton, and the Woman, looking at the blade-bone, heard him, and laughed, and said, "Here comes the first. Wild Thing out of the Wild Woods, what do you want?"

Wild Dog said, "O my Enemy and Wife of my Enemy, what is this that smells so good in the Wild Woods?"

Then the Woman picked up a roasted mutton-bone and threw

it to Wild Dog, and said, "Wild Thing out of the Wild Woods, taste and try." Wild Dog gnawed the bone, and it was more delicious than anything he had ever tasted, and he said, "O my Enemy and Wife of my Enemy, give me another."

The Woman said, "Wild Thing out of the Wild Woods, help my Man to hunt through the day and guard this Cave at night, and I will give you as many roast bones as you need."

"Ah!" said the Cat, listening. "This is a very wise Woman, but she is not so wise as I am."

Wild Dog crawled into the Cave and laid his head on the Woman's lap, and said, "O my Friend and Wife of my Friend, I will help your Man to hunt through the day, and at night I will guard your Cave."

"Ah!" said the Cat, listening. "That is a very foolish Dog." And he went back through the Wet Wild Woods waving his wild tail, and walking by his wild lone. But he never told anybody.

When the Man waked up he said, "What is Wild Dog doing here?" And the Woman said, "His name is not Wild Dog any more but the First Friend, because he will be our friend for always and always and always. Take him with you when you go hunting."

Next night the Woman cut great green armfuls of fresh grass from the water-meadows, and dried it before the fire, so that it smelt like new-mown hay, and she sat at the mouth of the Cave and plaited a halter out of horse-hide, and she looked at the shoulder of mutton bone—at the big broad blade-bone—and she made a Magic. She made the Second Singing Magic in the world.

Out in the Wild Woods all the

wild animals wondered what had happened to Wild Dog, and at last Wild Horse stamped with his foot and said, "I will go and see and say why Wild Dog has not returned. Cat, come with me."

"Nenni!" said the Cat. "I am the Cat who walks by himself, and all places are alike to me. I will not come." But all the same he followed Wild Horse softly, very softly, and hid himself where he could hear everything.

When the Woman heard Wild Horse tripping and stumbling on his long mane, she laughed and said, "Here comes the second. Wild Thing out of the Wild Woods, what do you want?"

Wild Horse said, "O my Enemy and Wife of my Enemy, where is Wild Dog?"

The Woman laughed, and picked up the blade-bone and looked at it, and said, "Wild Thing out of the Wild Woods,

you did not come here for Wild Dog, but for the sake of this good grass."

And Wild Horse, tripping and stumbling on his long mane, said, "That is true; give it me to eat."

The Woman said, "Wild Thing out of the Wild Woods, bend your wild head and wear what I give you, and you shall eat the wonderful grass three times a day."

"Ah," said the Cat, listening, "this is a clever Woman, but she is not so clever as I am."

Wild Horse bent his wild head, and the Woman slipped the plaited hide halter over it, and Wild Horse breathed on the Woman's feet and said, "O my Mistress, and Wife of my Master, I will be your servant for the sake of the wonderful grass."

"Ah," said the Cat, listening, "that is a very foolish Horse." And he went back through the Wet Wild Woods, waving his

wild tail and walking by his wild lone. But he never told anybody.

When the Man and the Dog came back from hunting, the Man said, "What is Wild Horse doing here?" And the Woman said, "His name is not Wild Horse any more, but the First Servant, because he will carry us from place to place for always and always and always. Ride on his back when you go hunting."

Next day, holding her wild head high that her wild horns should not catch in the wild trees, Wild Cow came up to the Cave, and the Cat followed, and hid himself just the same as before; and everything happened just the same as before; and the Cat said the same things as before, and when Wild Cow had promised to give her milk to the Woman every day in exchange for the wonderful grass, the Cat went back through the Wet Wild Woods waving his wild tail and walking by his wild lone, just

the same as before. But he never told anybody. And when the Man and the Horse and the Dog came home from hunting and asked the same questions same as before, the Woman said, "Her name is not Wild Cow any more, but the Giver of Good Food. She will give us the warm white milk for always and always and always, and I will take care of her while you and the First Friend and the First Servant go hunting."

Next day the Cat waited to see if any other Wild Thing would go up to the Cave, but no one moved in the Wet Wild Woods, so the Cat walked there by himself; and he saw the Woman milking the Cow, and he saw the light of the fire in the Cave, and he smelt the smell of the warm white milk.

Cat said, "O my Enemy and Wife of my Enemy, where did Wild Cow go?"

The Woman laughed and said, "Wild Thing out of the Wild Woods, go back to the Woods again, for I have braided up my

151

hair, and I have put away the magic blade-bone, and we have no more need of either friends or servants in our Cave."

Cat said, "I am not a friend, and I am not a servant. I am the Cat who walks by himself, and I wish to come into your cave."

Woman said, "Then why did you not come with First Friend on the first night?"

Cat grew very angry and said, "Has Wild Dog told tales of me?"

Then the Woman laughed and said, "You are the Cat who walks by himself, and all places are alike to you. You are neither a friend nor a servant. You have said it yourself. Go away and walk by yourself in all places alike."

Then Cat pretended to be sorry and said, "Must I never come into the Cave? Must I never sit by the warm fire? Must I never drink the warm white milk? You are very wise and very beautiful. You should not be cruel even to a Cat."

Woman said, "I knew I was wise, but I did not know I was beautiful. So I will make a bargain with you. If ever I say one word in your praise you may come into the Cave."

"And if you say two words in my praise?" said the Cat.

"I never shall," said the Woman, "but if I say two words in your praise, you may sit by the fire in the Cave."

"And if you say three words?" said the Cat.

"I never shall," said the Woman, "but if I say three words in your praise, you may drink the warm white milk three times a day for always and always and always."

Then the Cat arched his back and said, "Now let the Curtain at the mouth of the Cave, and the Fire at the back of the Cave, and the Milk-pots that stand beside the Fire, remember what my Enemy and the Wife of my Enemy has said." And he went away

The Cat That
Walked by Himself

through the Wet Wild Woods waving his wild tail and walking by his wild lone.

That night when the Man and the Horse and the Dog came home from hunting, the Woman did not tell them of the bargain that she had made with the Cat, because she was afraid that they might not like it.

Cat went far and far away and hid himself in the Wet Wild Woods by his wild lone for a long time till the Woman forgot all about him. Only the Bat—the little upside-down Bat—that hung inside the Cave, knew where Cat hid; and every evening Bat would fly to Cat with news of what was happening.

One evening Bat said, "There is a Baby in the Cave.

He is new and pink and fat and small, and the Woman is very fond of him."

"Ah," said the Cat, listening, "but what is the Baby fond of?"

"He is fond of things that are soft and tickle," said the Bat. "He is fond of warm things to hold in his arms when he goes to sleep. He is fond of being played with. He is fond of all those things."

"Ah," said the Cat, listening, "then my time has come."

Next night Cat walked through the Wet Wild Woods and hid very near the Cave till morning-time, and Man and Dog and Horse went hunting. The Woman was busy cooking that morning, and the Baby cried and interrupted. So she carried him outside the Cave and gave him a handful of pebbles to play with. But still the Baby cried.

153

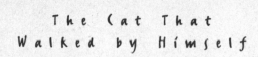

Then the Cat put out his paddy paw and patted the Baby on the cheek, and it cooed; and the Cat rubbed against its fat knees and tickled it under its fat chin with his tail. And the Baby laughed and the Woman heard him and smiled.

Then the Bat—the little upside-down Bat—that hung in the mouth of the Cave said, "O my Hostess and Wife of my Host and Mother of my Host's Son, a Wild Thing from the Wild Woods is most beautifully playing with your Baby."

"A blessing on that Wild Thing who-ever he may be," said the Woman, straightening her back, "for I was a busy woman this morning and he has done me a service."

That very minute and second, Best Beloved, the dried horse-skin Curtain that was stretched tail-down at the mouth of the Cave fell down—*woosh!*—because it remembered the bargain she had made with the Cat, and when the Woman went to pick it up—lo and behold!—the Cat was sitting quite comfy inside the Cave.

"O my Enemy and Wife of my Enemy and Mother of my Enemy," said the Cat, "it is I: for you have spoken a word in my praise, and now I can sit within the Cave for always and always and always. But still I am the Cat who walks by himself, and all places are alike to me."

The Woman was very angry, and shut her lips tight and took up her spinning-wheel and began to spin.

But the Baby cried because the Cat had gone away, and the Woman could not hush it, for it struggled and kicked and grew black in the face.

"O my Enemy and Wife of my Enemy and Mother of my Enemy," said the Cat, "take a strand of the wire that you are spinning and tie it to your spinning-whorl and drag it along the floor, and I will show you a Magic that shall make your Baby laugh as loudly as he is now crying."

"I will do so," said the Woman, "because I am at my wits' end; but I will not thank you for it."

She tied the thread to the little clay spindle-whorl and drew it across the floor, and the Cat ran after it and patted it with his paws and rolled head over heels, and tossed it backward over his shoulder and chased it between his hind-legs and pretended to lose it, and pounced down upon it again, till the Baby laughed as loudly as it had been crying, and scrambled after the Cat and frolicked all over the Cave till it grew tired and settled down to sleep with the Cat in its arms.

"Now," said the Cat, "I will sing the Baby a song that shall keep him asleep for an hour." And he began to purr, loud and low, low and loud, till the Baby fell fast asleep. The Woman smiled as she looked down upon the two of them and said, "That was wonderfully done. No question but you are very clever, O Cat."

That very minute and second, Best Beloved, the smoke of the fire at the back of the Cave came down in clouds from the roof—*puff!*—because it remembered the bargain she had made with the Cat, and when it had cleared away—

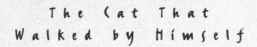

The Cat That Walked by Himself

lo and behold!—the Cat was sitting quite comfy close to the fire.

"O my Enemy and Wife of my Enemy and Mother of my Enemy," said the Cat, "it is I, for you have spoken a second word in my praise, and now I can sit by the warm fire at the back of the Cave for always and always and always. But still I am the Cat who walks by himself, and all places are alike to me."

Then the Woman was very very angry, and let down her hair and put more wood on the fire and brought out the broad blade-bone of the shoulder of mutton and began to make a Magic that should prevent her from saying a third word in praise of the Cat. It was not a Singing Magic, Best Beloved, it was a Still Magic; and by and by the Cave grew so still that a little wee-

wee mouse crept out of a corner and ran across the floor.

"O my Enemy and Wife of my Enemy and Mother of my Enemy," said the Cat, "is that little mouse part of your magic?"

"Ouh! Chee! No indeed!" said the Woman, and she dropped the blade-bone and jumped upon the footstool in front of the fire and braided up her hair very quick for fear that the mouse should run up it.

"Ah," said the Cat, watching, "then the mouse will do me no harm if I eat it?"

"No," said the Woman, braiding up her hair, "eat it quickly and I will ever be grateful to you."

Cat made one jump and caught the little mouse, and the Woman said, "A hundred thanks. Even the First Friend is not quick enough to catch little mice as you have done. You must be very wise."

That very moment and second, O Best Beloved,

156

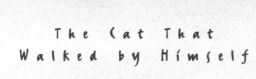

The Cat That Walked by Himself

the Milk-pot that stood by the fire cracked in two pieces—*ffft*—because it remembered the bargain she had made with the Cat, and when the Woman jumped down from the footstool—lo and behold!—the Cat was lapping up the warm white milk that lay in one of the broken pieces.

"O my Enemy and Wife of my Enemy and Mother of my Enemy," said the Cat, "it is I; for you have spoken three words in my praise, and now I can drink the warm white milk three times a day for always and always and always. But *still* I am the cat who walks by himself, and all places are alike to me."

Then the Woman laughed and set the Cat a bowl of the warm white milk and said, "O Cat, you are as clever as a man, but remember that your bargain was not made with the Man or the Dog, and I do not know what they will do when they come home."

"What is that to me?" said the Cat. "If I have my place in the Cave by the fire and my warm white milk three times a day I do not care what the Man or the Dog can do."

That evening when the Man and the Dog came into the Cave, the Woman told them all the story of the bargain while the Cat sat by the fire and smiled. Then the Man said, "Yes, but he has not made a bargain with *me* or with all proper Men after me." Then he took off his two leather boots and he took up his little stone axe (that makes three) and he fetched a piece of wood and a hatchet (that is five altogether), and he set them out in a row and he

157

said, "Now we will make *our* bargain. If you do not catch mice when you are in the Cave for always and always and always, I will throw these five things at you whenever I see you, and so shall all proper Men do after me."

"Ah," said the Woman, listening, "this is a very clever Cat, but he is not so clever as my Man."

The Cat counted the five things (and they looked very knobby) and he said, "I will catch mice when I am in the Cave for always and always and always; but *still* I am the Cat who walks by himself, and all places are alike to me."

"Not when I am near," said the Man. "If you had not said that last I would have put all these things away for always and always and always; but I am now going to throw my two boots and my little stone axe (that makes three) at you whenever I meet you. And so shall all proper Men do after me!"

Then the Dog said, "Wait a minute. He has not made a bargain with *me* or with all proper Dogs after me." And he showed his teeth and said, "If you are not kind to the Baby while I am in the Cave for always and always and always, I will hunt you till I catch you, and when I catch you I will bite you. And so shall all proper Dogs do after me."

"Ah," said the Woman, listening, "this is a very clever Cat, but he is not so clever as the Dog."

Cat counted the Dog's teeth (and they looked very pointed) and he said, "I will be kind to the Baby while I am in the Cave, as long as he does not pull my tail too hard, for always and always and always. But *still* I am the Cat that walks by himself, and all places are alike to me."

"Not when I am near," said the Dog. "If you had not said that last I would have shut my mouth for always and always and always, but *now* I am going to hunt you up a tree whenever I meet you. And so shall all proper Dogs do after me."

Then the Man threw his two boots and his little stone axe (that makes three) at the Cat, and the Cat ran out of the Cave, and the Dog chased him up a tree; and from that day to this, Best Beloved, three proper Men out of five will always throw things at a Cat whenever they meet him, and all proper Dogs will chase him up a tree. But the Cat keeps his side of the bargain too. He will kill mice and he will be kind to Babies when he is in the house, just as long as they do not pull his tail too hard. But when he has done that, and between times, and when the moon gets up and night comes, he is the Cat that walks by himself, and all places are alike to him. Then he goes out to the Wet Wild Woods or up the Wet Wild Trees or on the Wet Wild Roofs, waving his tail and walking by his wild lone.

Have a miniature fur ball who seems more like a pouncing cactus with teeth than a soft, sweet feline? Kittenproof your hands with oven mitts for playtime. Many young ones are so full of energy, they don't know what to do with it all. They also are teething and need to chew. Kittens usually outgrow this phase, with some of the biggest roughhousers turning into the most attentive companions. Play aggression—even attacking your feet—most commonly occurs in young cats left alone for much of the day. The answer is: Play with your cat!

Kitty Attack

Make a pet first-aid kit. It should contain:

Phone numbers of your vet, poison control center, and 24-hour animal hospital • Styptic powder for a bleeding claw • Gauze to wrap wounds or muzzle an injured pet (do not muzzle if vomiting) • Roll of stretchy, self-sticking bandaging material • Adhesive tape • Nonstick sterile pads • Tweezers and small scissors (blunt-ended) • Rectal thermometer and petroleum jelly • Towel • Hydrogen peroxide • Triple antibiotic ointment • Eyewash • Cotton pads • Food syringe or eyedropper for oral medications.

Clicker Training Step 3
Capturing

Newbie clicker folks love *capturing*—marking and rewarding a behavior a subject offers on his own—and sitting, pawing, stretching, and rolling are perfect natural cat behaviors to use. In addition, you can *shape* or modify a captured behavior in tiny increments: A cat who knows the Gimme Five can learn to have his claws trimmed without fussing! Work on one behavior at a time before teaching a new one; don't combine them. All it takes is a couple of two- or three-minute sessions per day.

clicker, 20 or so treats per session

Sit

1. You can teach this while sitting on the couch or standing in front of your cat. Put her on the floor and observe her. Eventually she will decide to sit. As her hindquarters descend to the floor, *click!*—and treat. You have captured a behavior.
2. Nudge her gently to a standing position with your foot if you need to. Every time she starts to sit, click and treat, and repeat. Add the cue, "Sit," just as she is getting ready to do it. Remember, click while the butt is hitting the floor, not after.
3. When you start the second session later that day or the next

one, the cat will have to backtrack a little—but she'll catch on faster the second time around.

4. After about 20 short sessions spread out over, say, 10 days, your cat should sit fairly consistently when you say the cue (but don't expect her to do this in the presence of guests or distractions—this takes a while!).

Gimme Five

1. Wiggle your fist around on the floor in front of your cat. Eventually he will lift a paw or touch your hand. Capture any movement of a paw, even if tentative, with a well-timed *click!*—and treat. Don't ask for a pat at first.

2. Once your cat touches your hand repeatedly for a CT (click and treat), stick your hand out flat on the floor and say, "Gimme five." (Make sure you offer a hand that has not been holding treats, or your cat will sniff instead of pat.) CT a paw movement. It will become a pat with practice. Do not CT for sniffing, or your cat will learn the wrong thing.

3. After you and your cat have nailed this trick, raise your hand a little higher for dramatic effect. Now you are starting to *shape* the behavior.

VARIATION: Want your friends to think your cat can count? Hold your hand above your cat's head and say, "Gimme ten!" Most cats will sit up and place both paws against it.

Puff Muffins

Looking for a nourishing between-meal treat for your cat? Combine the chewy texture of nutritious oatmeal with the salty flavor of chicken broth, and you'll have a snack fit for a king's court at teatime. Puss in Boots would love these.

$1^1/_2$ cups rolled oats
$^1/_2$ cup flour
$^1/_4$ cup corn oil
$^1/_2$ cup chicken broth

1. Preheat the oven to 350°F.
2. Combine all ingredients in a large bowl. Flour your hands and knead until thoroughly mixed.
3. Form the mixture into tiny bite-size muffins and drop onto a greased cookie sheet.
4. Bake for about 15 minutes, or until lightly browned. Store the treats in a sealed container for up to 2 weeks.

Makes about 4–5 cups of treats.

A cat is always on the wrong side of the door.

—Anonymous

The Roaming Cat

by Adlai Stevenson

State of Illinois
Executive Department
Springfield, April 23, 1949

To the Honorable, the Members of the Senate of the 66th General Assembly:

I herewith return, without my approval, Senate Bill No. 93 entitled "An Act to Provide Protection to Insectivorous Birds by Restraining Cats." This is the so-called "Cat Bill." I veto and withhold my approval from this Bill for the following reasons:

It would impose fines on owners or keepers who permitted their cats to run at large off their premises. It would permit any person to capture, or call upon the police to pick up and imprison, cats at large. . . . This legislation has been introduced in the past several sessions of the Legislature, and it has, over the years, been the source of much comment—not all of which has been in a serious vein. . . . I cannot believe there is a widespread public demand for this law or that it could, as a practical matter, be enforced.

Furthermore, I cannot agree that it should be the declared public policy of Illinois that a cat visiting a neighbor's yard or crossing the highway is a public nuisance. It is in the nature of cats to do a certain amount of unescorted roaming. . . . Also consider the owner's dilemma: To escort a cat abroad on a leash is against the nature of the cat, and to permit it to venture forth for exercise unattended into a night of new dangers is against the nature of the owner. Moreover, cats perform useful service, particularly in rural areas, in combating rodents—work they necessarily perform alone and without regard for property lines. . . .

The problem of cat *versus* bird is as old as time. If we attempt to resolve it by legislation who knows but what we may be called upon to take sides as well in the age-old problem of dog *versus* cat, bird *versus* bird, or even bird *versus* worm. In my opinion, the State of Illinois and its local governing bodies already have enough to do without trying to control feline delinquency.

For these reasons, and not because I love birds the less or cats the more, I veto and withhold my approval from Senate Bill No. 93.

Respectfully,
Adlai E. Stevenson, Governor

The Owl and the Pussy-cat

by Edward Lear

The Owl and the Pussy-cat went to sea
   In a beautiful pea-green boat,
They took some honey, and plenty of money,
   Wrapped up in a five-pound note.
The Owl looked up to the stars above,
   And sang to a small guitar,
"O lovely Pussy! O Pussy, my love,
   What a beautiful Pussy you are,
            You are,
            You are!
What a beautiful Pussy you are!"

Pussy said to the Owl, "You elegant fowl!
   How charmingly sweet you sing!

171

O let us be married! too long have we tarried:
      But what *shall* we do for a ring!"
They sailed away, for a year and a day,
      To the land where the Bong-tree grows,
And there in a wood a Piggy-wig *stood*
      With a ring at the end of his nose,
                  His nose,
                  His nose,
      With a ring at the end of his nose.

"Dear Pig, are you willing to sell for one shilling
      Your ring?" Said the Piggy, "I will."
So they took it away, and were married next day
      By the Turkey who lives on the hill.
They dined on mince, and slices of quince,
      Which they ate with a runcible spoon;
And hand in hand, on the edge of the sand,
      They danced by the light of the moon,
                  The moon,
                  The moon,
They danced by the light of the moon.

Feline Funnies

Cat Fancy

A tom cat and a tabby cat were courting on a roof at night. The tom leaned over toward the tabby with pent-up passion and purred, "I'll die for you!"

The tabby gazed at him with narrowed eyes and asked, "How many times?"

Cute as a Kitten

A three-year-old boy went with his dad to see a new litter of kittens. On returning home, he breathlessly informed his mother, "There were two boy kittens and two girl kittens." "How did you know that?" his mother asked. "Daddy picked them up and looked underneath," he replied. "I think it's printed on the bottom."

TRASH TALKIN' A large cat communicates his size, and therefore his dominance, to other cats in his range by stretching to his full height and placing scratch marks on trees.

OUCH! The cat's nervous system is very similar to ours, and cats experience pain in much the same way people do. Pain-relief medications after surgery are considered essential.

RADAR A cat's ear has more than a dozen muscles, which can rotate it up to 180 degrees.

BUILT FOR SPEED All cats are programmed to chase anything that moves. Cheetahs—the fastest animals on earth—cannot help but chase a big, furry toy that runs on a drag strip, allowing scientists to clock their acceleration at 0 to 60 in five seconds.

Feline Facts

NINE LIVES AND FORTY WINKS Cats can sleep up to 16 hours per day—18 in hot climates.

I KNEAD YOU A kitten learns to knead her mama's stomach to milk her assigned teat for all it's worth. Forever linked to pleasure, kneading recurs during mating and in the form of stomping the ground before pouncing on prey.

CATICURE Scratching pulls the horny sheath off cats' claws and allows for proper retraction.

ON THE HUNT Feral cat mothers carry home still-alive prey—ideally a mouse—to their offspring, and show them how to administer a killing bite. Uneducated house cats are notoriously inefficient at finishing the job.

CATCH THE BUZZ Blind, newborn kittens first hear their mama's loud purring as a dinner call. Like kneading, purring recurs with pleasure, but can occur during fright as well.

NATURAL HIGH *Catnip contains a compound that smells to a cat like a female in heat.*

LATE SHOW Cats love it when their human stays up to watch television, sometimes going on late-night activity sprees. Although not nocturnal, their perfect meal (a mouse) is, so they arrange their schedule accordingly.

BALANCING ACT Cats use the bottoms of the paws, skin, eyes, tail, inner ear, and brain to position themselves in space—and land on their feet.

PLAYACTING Cats instinctively play to sharpen their hunting skills, even when not hungry.

Obstacle Course

While dog agility and equestrian competitions have been in existence for many years, International Cat Agility Tournaments (ICAT) premiered in Albuquerque, New Mexico, in October 2003.

Training animals to complete a course in the correct order relies on a concept called backchaining, in which a number of learned behaviors are strung together. Agility courses comprise pieces of gym equipment for animals. But you don't have to do anything fancy to set up a "cat gym" at home. You can construct most of the elements out of materials such as cardboard boxes, pillows, and plastic cups. Arrange them in a circuit around the room. Use clicker training to help your cat to complete the obstacle course.

Pedestal You might begin your gym workout by asking your cat to jump up and sit on a small stool for a treat. If your cat knows Touch (page 84), you can use this to signal, "Playtime begins!"

Tunnels Indispensable to obstacle-course lovers, these can be bought ready-made or taped together from cardboard cartons.

Weave Course Place four or five upside-down cups or stacking plastic children's cones in a row on the floor and teach your cat to weave back and forth through them by having her follow a toy or the chopstick you use for Touch.

Ramp Build a slight incline up to a small table using a piece of wood, some sturdy cardboard, or a pillow. Secure an old towel around the ramp. The cat can run up the ramp and jump off the other end of the table onto a padded or carpeted surface as part of the course.

Hurdle Incorporate a hop over a hurdle (page 224).

The Cheshire-Cat

by Lewis Carroll

The Cat only grinned when it saw Alice. It looked good-natured, she thought: still it had *very* long claws and a great many teeth, so she felt that it ought to be treated with respect.

"Cheshire-Puss," she began, rather timidly, as she did not at all know whether it would like the name: however, it only grinned a little wider. "Come, it's pleased so far," thought Alice, and she went on. "Would you tell me, please, which way I ought to go from here?"

"That depends a good deal on where you want to get to," said the Cat.

"I don't much care where—" said Alice.

"Then it doesn't matter which way you go," said the Cat.

"—so long as I get *somewhere*," Alice added as an explanation.

"Oh, you're sure to do that," said the Cat, "if you only walk long enough."

Alice felt that this could not be denied, so she tried another question. "What sort of people live about here?"

"In *that* direction," the Cat said, waving its right paw round, "lives a Hatter: and in *that* direction," waving the other paw, "lives a March Hare. Visit either you like: they're both mad."

"But I don't want to go among mad people," Alice remarked.

"Oh, you ca'n't help that," said the Cat: "we're all mad here. I'm mad. You're mad."

"How do you know I'm mad?" said Alice.

"You must be," said the Cat, "or you wouldn't have come here."

Alice didn't think that proved

it at all: however, she went on: "And how do you know that you're mad?"

"To begin with," said the Cat, "a dog's not mad. You grant that."

"I suppose so," said Alice.

"Well, then," the Cat went on, "you see a dog growls when it's angry, and wags its tail when it's pleased. Now *I* growl when I'm pleased, and wag my tail when I'm angry. Therefore I'm mad."

"*I* call it purring, not growling," said Alice.

"Call it what you like," said the Cat. "Do you play croquet with the Queen to-day?"

"I should like it very much," said Alice, "but I haven't been invited yet."

"You'll see me there," said the Cat, and vanished.

Alice was not much surprised at this, she was getting so well used to queer things

happening. While she was still looking at the place where it had been, it suddenly appeared again.

"By-the-bye, what became of the baby?" said the Cat. "I'd nearly forgotten to ask."

"It turned into a pig," Alice answered very quietly, just as if the Cat had come back in a natural way.

"I thought it would," said the Cat, and vanished again.

Alice waited a little, half expecting to see it again, but it did not appear, and after a minute or two she walked on in the direction in which the March Hare was said to live. "I've seen hatters before," she said to herself: "the March Hare will be much the most interesting, and perhaps, as this is May, it wo'n't be raving mad— at least not so mad as it was in March." As

she said this she looked up, and there was the Cat again, sitting on a branch of a tree.

"Did you say 'pig,' or 'fig'?" said the Cat.

"I said 'pig'," replied Alice; "and I wish you wouldn't keep appearing and vanishing so suddenly: you make one quite giddy!"

"All right," said the Cat; and this time it vanished quite slowly, beginning with the end of the tail, and ending with the grin, which remained some time after the rest of it had gone.

"Well! I've often seen a cat without a grin," thought Alice; "but a grin without a cat! It's the most curious thing I ever saw in all my life!"

nimals play an important role in fiction, even if only as nameless fireside companions. A book without at least one pet is a cold piece of fiction indeed—even Shakespeare had his Grimalkin. In the ragingly popular Harry Potter series, Hermione acquires a cat named Crookshanks, while Fitch's pet, the terrible Mrs. Norris, patrols the halls of Hogwarts. Mystery writer Rita Mae Brown gets help from feline co-writer Sneaky Pie Brown. The classics give us such well-known cat characters as the Cheshire Cat (Alice's Adventures in Wonderland), Figaro (Disney's version of Pinocchio), Sher Khan (The Jungle Book), and Tigger (Winnie-the-Pooh). Stephen King brings back to life the cat Church in Pet Sematary, while Capri was companion to the multiple personalities of Sybil's protagonist. And what could be a more perfect

Literary Cats

name for a lioness than Elsa, of Born Free? Finally, we wonder how many cat lovers have named their beloved pets after Don Marquis's famous Mehitabel, who claims to be a reincarnation of Cleopatra. Some wonderful felines jump out at us from literature:

LADY JANE, from Dickens's *Bleak House* • **CHATTIE**, from Mary Augusta Ward's *Robert Elsmere* • **WOTAN**, from Henry Handel Richardson's *Maurice Guest* • **MOUMOUTTE BLANCHE** and **MOUMOUTTE CHINOISE**, from Pierre Loti • **PUFF, MURR**, and **BRISQUET**, from Balzac • **FRANCHETTE, SAHA**, and **KIKI-LA-DOUCETTE**, from Colette • **ALEXANDER FURBY**, from Ursula K. Le Guin's *Wonderful Alexander and the Catwings* • **BLOOMBERG**, from J. D. Salinger's *Franny & Zooey* • **BUSTOPHER JONES**, from T. S. Eliot's *Old Possum's Book of Practical Cats* • **CATASAUQUA**, from Mark Twain's *Letters from the Earth* • **CHILDEBRAND, ENJORAS, SÉRAPHITA, ZIZI**, and **EPONINE**, from Théophile Gautier's *La Ménagerie Intime* • **EATBUGS, GRIZRAZ HEARTEATER, POUNCEQUICK**, and **FIRSA ROOFSHADOW**, from Tad Williams's *Tailchaser's Song* • **ITTY**, from Hugh Lofting's Dr. Dolittle books • **MIDNIGHT LOUIE** and **MIDNIGHT LOUISE**, from Carole Nelson Douglas's books • **MITTENS, MOPPET, PERCY, SIMPKIN, SQUINTINA, TABITHA TWITCHIT**, and **MRS. RIBBY**, from Beatrix Potter's books • **NITCHEVO**, from Tennessee Williams's story "The Malediction" • **PICKLES**, from Esther Averill's *Pickles the Fire Cat* • **PIXEL**, from Robert Heinlein's books • **PLUTO**, from Edgar Allan Poe's "The Black Cat" • **RHUBARB**, from H. Allen Smith's *Rhubarb* • **SIR GREEN-EYES GRIMALKIN DE TABBY DE SLY**, from Laura E. Richards's "The Sad Story of the Dandy Cat" • **TATTOO** and **PINKLE PURR**, from A. A. Milne's poem "Pinkle Purr" • **WEBSTER**, from P. G. Wodehouse's "The Story of Webster" • **ZAPAQUILDA**, from Lope de Vega's *The Battle of the Cats*.

The cat went here and there
And the moon spun round like a top,
And the nearest kin of the moon,
The creeping cat, looked up.
Black Minnaloushe stared at the moon,
For, wander and wail as he would,
The pure cold light in the sky
Troubled his animal blood.
Minnaloushe runs in the grass
Lifting his delicate feet.
Do you dance, Minnaloushe, do you dance?
When two close kindred meet,
What better than call a dance?
Maybe the moon may learn,
Tired of that courtly fashion,
A new dance turn.
Minnaloushe creeps through the grass
From moonlit place to place,
The sacred moon overhead
Has taken a new phase.
Does Minnaloushe know that his pupils

Will pass from change to change,
And that from round to crescent,
From crescent to round they range?
Minnaloushe creeps through the grass
Alone, important and wise,
And lifts to the changing moon
His changing eyes.

The Cat and the Moon

by
W. B. Yeats

Magic Box

Great for groups of cats, this simple activity takes advantage of the fact that cats love to sniff and rub any new object in their territory.

cardboard box, a clicker (or use a mouth click), treats or kibble

1. Place a lightweight cardboard carton in the middle of a space. Wait for your cat to notice the box. Make a clicking sound for any interaction, even if your cat just looks at the box from across the room. Then give or toss a treat. If your cat does not show increased interest, toss the box in the air; that often brings furry friends running. Also, consider changing to a tastier treat. Food talks.

2. Each time a cat sniffs, rubs, looks at, meows at, or touches the box in any way, click and treat. He will soon realize that he is being rewarded for having anything to do with the box, and will increase his interaction. If the cat is very active, give a treat after every few clicks.

3. Up the ante. As the cat keeps playing with the box, you might click and treat only when he jumps into or out of the box, or only when he rubs the box. (But don't make it so hard he gets frustrated and walks away!) As you click a particular behavior, the cat will offer that one behavior more often than any other. The cat is being subconsciously conditioned to offer a desired behavior through the rewards you give him. People learn and are socialized in the same way—through positive incentives.

4. Put the box away when you are done with your session; cats eventually become uninterested when it's left out and they stop getting treats.

The Science of Cats

LAW OF CAT INERTIA A cat at rest will tend to remain at rest, unless acted upon by some outside force—such as the opening of a cat food container, or a nearby scurrying mouse.

LAW OF CAT MAGNETISM All blue blazers and black sweaters attract cat hair in direct proportion to the darkness of the fabric.

LAW OF CAT SLEEPING All cats must sleep with people whenever possible, in a position as uncomfortable for the people involved as is possible for the cat.

LAW OF CAT ELONGATION A cat can make her body long enough to reach just about any countertop that has anything remotely interesting on it.

LAW OF CAT DISINTEREST A cat's interest level will vary in inverse proportion to the amount of effort a human expends in trying to interest him.

LAW OF OBEDIENCE RESISTANCE A cat's resistance varies in proportion to a human's desire for her to do something.

LAW OF PILL REJECTION Any pill given to a cat has the potential energy to reach escape velocity.

FIRST LAW OF ENERGY CONSERVATION Cats know that energy can neither be created nor destroyed. They will, therefore, use as little energy as possible.

SECOND LAW OF ENERGY CONSERVATION Cats also know that energy can only be stored by a lot of napping.

LAW OF REFRIGERATOR OBSERVATION If a cat watches a refrigerator long enough, someone will come along and take out something good to eat.

LAW OF RANDOM COMFORT SEEKING A cat will always seek, and usually take over, the most comfortable spot in any given room.

LAW OF FURNITURE REPLACEMENT A cat's desire to scratch furniture is directly proportional to the cost of the furniture.

LAW OF CAT COMPOSITION A cat is composed of Matter + Antimatter + It Doesn't Matter.

Cat Outing

One fine sunny day, two robins were lying on their backs, enjoying the sun. A mother cat and her kittens went strolling by. The kittens, as always, were saying how hungry they were and asking what they could have to eat. Their mama, spying the birds, said, "How about some baskin' robins?"

CAT TALES

Dick Whittington was a poor boy who lived in the English countryside. He had been orphaned at a young age and had no relatives to speak of. He spent his days scrabbling for a bit to eat, and trying desperately to find a place to sleep each night.

One day, he overheard a man telling his friend about the wondrous city of London. He spoke of how the streets were paved with gold, and how any young man who was willing to work hard would become a gentleman there in no time at all.

Dick Whittington and his Wonderful Cat

An English Tale

"Why, if that's so, I can pry up a bit of cobblestone and be fed for the next month!" Dick thought, "There is nothing for me in this village. I will try my luck in London!" And the very next day he set off on the road

to the city. Moving was very easy for him, as he had no possessions but the shirt on his back and the hope in his heart.

After trekking the long, long road, Dick could just make out the twisted spires and tall buildings of London. And from far away, it did look like a magical place.

But when Dick arrived in the city, he found a very different world than he'd imagined. Instead of gold paving the streets, there were mountains of garbage and waste. Smoke and odor hung in the air, and a million horrible noises fell upon his ears. Dick was afraid, but he had nowhere else to go. So he set about trying to find employment in one of the houses nearby. As his luck would have it, Dick found a job right at his first stop, for that very day a kitchen boy had run away from the Fitzwarren household.

Unfortunately for Dick, the kitchen boy had a good reason to run away: the Fitzwarren kitchen was run by the most mean-hearted cook. All day long she tormented poor Dick, calling him lazy, filthy, and any other horrible insult she could think of. She was never far behind him with a curse on her lips and a frying pan in her hand. She even boarded him in the most rat-plagued room in the house.

CAT TALES

"You should be used to rooming with vermin by now," she snorted.

All night long, Dick could hardly sleep due to the small army of mice marching over his bed. But Dick was not ready to give up yet. He began to save up his money, and the first chance he got, he bought a beautiful little tabby cat. Everyone in the house adored her.

"What a sweet little kitten," Fitzwarren's daughter, Sophie, exclaimed, and she spent a great deal of time playing with Dick and his new pet whenever his kitchen duties were done. The cat proved to be a terrific mouser, and Dick's room quickly became the only place in the house that did not host a mouse or two. With his new pet and a pest-free bed, Dick found it easier to bear the cruelties of the horrible cook.

As the years passed, Dick Whittington grew into a strong young man. He worked hard for Mr. Fitzwarren, but no matter what he did, the cook never let up her torrent of abuse. It made life hard for Dick, but he managed to be cheered every time he returned to his dear cat.

The cat, too, had blossomed. She became a large, sleek cat who kept the house free of all kinds of mice and vermin. She was so good at her job that the family sometimes good-naturedly grumbled about oversleeping.

They had a tendency to stay in their beds, since they no longer had the nibbling and scratching of mice to keep them awake at night.

One day, Mr. Fitzwarren called his family and servants together for an important announcement. One of his merchant ships would soon be making a trip to the dark coast of Africa, a port that he had never attempted before.

"I would like all of my servants to be given a chance to earn their good fortune, so I propose that each of you send something on this boat to trade," he told them. All of the servants were excited at the prospect of making some money, and they set about finding their most valuable item to trade.

All that is, except for poor Dick Whittington, who had nothing more than his clothes and his health. "Dear Dick," Sophie asked him, "why do you look so upset?"

"I have nothing to send on this fine voyage," he said, with shame in his eyes, "for I own nothing in the world except for my cat."

Fitzwarren had been listening close by, and he clapped Dick on the shoulder. "Well, why don't you think about

sending along your cat? We all know that she is a fine mouser. I'm certain she will keep the ship clear of any pests that may want to get on board."

Dick was reluctant to let his little cat go, as she was his dearest friend in the world, but he did want to make something of himself. Finally, he gave his consent to send her on the journey.

After his cat was gone, Dick was more miserable than ever. The cook seemed crueler than she had ever been before, and even Sophie could not cheer him up. After an especially bad assault from the cook one evening, Dick decided he had had enough of the Fitzwarren household and ran away. He was halfway down the street, when he suddenly heard the bells of London ringing. Now, he had heard them ring on more times than he could think of, but for some reason, this time they seemed to be saying, "Turn again, Whittington, Lord Mayor of London!"

"I don't believe my ears!" Dick thought, "Could I really be Lord Mayor one day?" He didn't think that dream would ever come true, but he did resolve to turn back and try his luck again at the Fitzwarren household.

Months passed, and things stayed relatively the same, until one day, Sophie came running into the kitchen. "Quick, Father sent me to fetch

CAT TALES

you, Dick! He said he has a wonderful surprise for you at the ships!" He followed her as quickly as lightning to the docks, where he saw Fitzwarren overseeing the unloading of cargo. Almost before he knew it, a tiny orange shape darted over the deck and leapt into his arms! It was his beautiful cat, alive and purring next to his heart!

"This is the most wonderful surprise ever!" Dick shouted, but Fitzwarren interrupted his reunion. "I am glad to see you so happy, Dick, but she's not the surprise I was talking about!" He gave a signal and barrel after barrel of gold coins were rolled out and placed in front of Dick.

"To whom do these riches belong ?" Dick whispered in awe.

"Why," replied Fitzwarren, "to you, my son."

He explained that when the captain and crew arrived in Africa, they were met by a nobleman and his wife and invited to dinner. But when they sat down at the meal, they were barely able to salvage a crumb. You see, mice had completely overrun their household, and due to a strange sickness that had swept through the village, they had no cats to deter them! The captain immediately thought of Dick's cat, and brought her to the house, where she proceeded to wreak havoc on the mouse population.

CAT TALES

The noble couple was so taken by her that they let her sleep on a pillow of silk, and rewarded her with tubs of cream to drink. Dick's cat settled down, and even had a litter of kittens that turned out to be just as excellent at hunting mice as their mother was. When the time came to leave, the kittens became the royal pets of the household, and the couple totaled up the entire sum of the cargo of the ship, and then doubled it as payment for what Dick's cat had done!

And so Dick got his cat back and became very wealthy in the process. He used his money towards an education and built his own fine merchant business. He became a very successful gentleman in his time, and eventually asked for the hand of Sophie Fitzwarren in marriage. The happy couple lived at the house for a great many years, and Dick was voted Lord Mayor of London, not once, but twice!

Dick Whittington never forgot how he owed his fortune to one small cat. And Dick's cat, in turn, repaid his love by keeping his house completely free of mice until the end of her days.

What's for Dinner?

The pet food industry falls under the jurisdiction of the Food and Drug Administration (FDA). Consumers should be as concerned about what's in the formulations they feed their animals as they are about their own food. Some even shun commercially processed food altogether, feeding their cats bones and raw food (BARF). You'll want to read the label on any commercially produced pet food. Make sure it states that it has passed the AAFCO's (Association of American Feed Control Officials) standardized feeding trials, and keep in mind that ingredients are listed in order by weight.

Making homemade cat food with the proper balance of nutrients is a very tricky business, and should not be attempted without a vet's supervision. To insure that your cat does not develop deficiencies, feed him a high-quality cat food and use the recipes in this book as occasional treats only. Never feed him dog food: Cats require a higher level of protein than dogs.

Do not use cows' milk as a substitute for water. Milk contains lactose, which some cats find difficult to digest. Consuming large quantities may not be well tolerated and can cause diarrhea.

Lamb and Rice Delight

Lamb and rice are both popular cat food ingredients. Here's a healthy snack that appeals to your feline's fondness for protein and fat, with a little extra "zing" thrown in.

4 ounces ground lamb
1/4 cup cooked rice
2 tablespoons cornmeal
1 egg
1 teaspoon catnip
dash of salt

1. Preheat the broiler to 425°F. Combine all the ingredients and knead the mixture into a ball.
2. Place on a greased cookie sheet and flatten to a thickness of about 1/2 inch.
3. Broil for 4 minutes on each side, or until crisp. Let it cool for 30 minutes.
4. Cut into small treat-size pieces. These will keep for up to a week in a sealed container in the refrigerator.

Makes about 6 dozen treats.

She sights a Bird—she chuckles—
She flattens—then she crawls—
She runs without the look of feet—
Her eyes increase to Balls—

Her Jaws stir—twitching—hungry—
Her Teeth can hardly stand—
She leaps, but Robin leaped the first—
Ah, Pussy, of the Sand,

The Hopes so juicy ripening—
You almost bathed your Tongue—
When Bliss disclosed a hundred Toes—
And fled with every one—

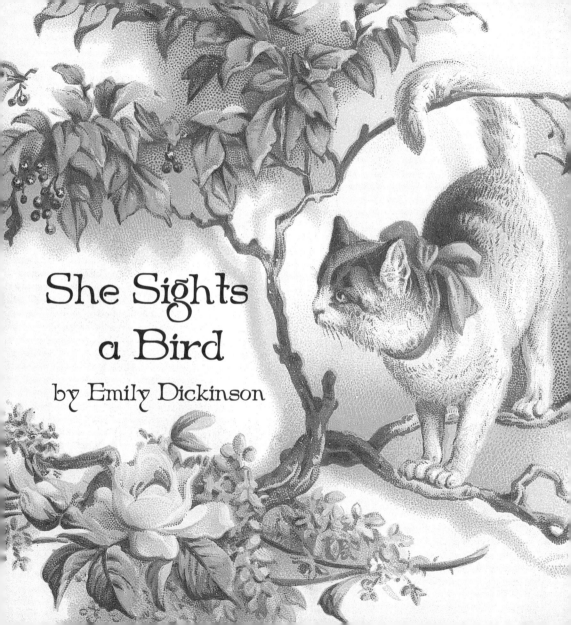

She Sights a Bird

by Emily Dickinson

The cat loves fish... but does
not like to wet her paws.

— ENGLISH PROVERB

Cat in the Rain

by Ernest Hemingway

There were only two Americans stopping at the hotel. They did not know any of the people they passed on the stairs on their way to and from their room. Their room was on the second floor facing the sea. It also faced the public garden and the war monument. There were big palms and green benches in the public garden. In the good weather there was always an artist with his easel. Artists liked the way the palms grew and the bright colors of the hotels facing the gardens and the sea. Italians came from a long way off to look up at the war monument. It was made of bronze and glistened in the rain. It was raining. The rain dripped from the palm trees. Water stood in pools on the gravel paths. The sea broke in a long line in the rain and slipped back down the beach to come up and break again in a long line in the rain. The motor cars were gone from the square by the war monument. Across the square in the doorway of the café a waiter stood looking out at the empty square.

The American wife stood at the window looking out. Outside right under their window a cat was crouched under one of the dripping green tables. The cat was trying to make herself so compact that she would not be dripped on.

"I'm going down and get that kitty," the American wife said.

"I'll do it," her husband offered from the bed.

"No, I'll get it. The poor kitty out trying to keep dry under a table."

The husband went on reading, lying propped up with the two pillows at the foot of the bed.

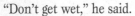

Cat in the Rain

"Don't get wet," he said.

The wife went downstairs and the hotel owner stood up and bowed to her as she passed the office. His desk was at the far end of the office. He was an old man and very tall.

"Il poive," the wife said. She liked the hotel-keeper.

"Si, si, Signora, brutto tempo. It's very bad weather."

He stood behind his desk in the far end of the dim room. The wife liked him. She liked the deadly serious way he received any complaints. She liked his dignity. She liked the way he wanted to serve her. She liked the way he felt about being a hotel-keeper. She liked his old, heavy face and big hands.

Liking him she opened the door and looked out. It was raining harder. A man in a rubber cape was crossing the empty square to the café. The cat would be around to the right. Perhaps she could go along under the eaves. As she stood in the doorway an umbrella opened behind her. It was the maid who looked after their room.

"You must not get wet," she smiled, speaking Italian. Of course, the hotel-keeper had sent her.

With the maid holding the umbrella over her, she walked along the gravel path until she was under their window. The table was there, washed bright green in the rain, but the cat was gone. She was suddenly disappointed. The maid looked up at her.

"Ha perduto qualque cosa, Signora?"

"There was a cat," said the American girl.

"A cat?"

"Si, il gatto."

"A cat?" the maid laughed. "A cat in the rain?"

"Yes," she said, "under the table." Then, "Oh, I wanted it so much. I wanted a kitty."

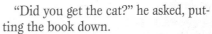

Cat in the Rain

When she talked English the maid's face tightened.

"Come, Signora," she said. "We must get back inside. You will be wet."

"I suppose so," said the American girl.

They went back along the gravel path and passed in the door. The maid stayed outside to close the umbrella. As the American girl passed the office, the padrone bowed from his desk. Something felt very small and tight inside the girl. The padrone made her feel very small and at the same time really important. She had a momentary feeling of being of supreme importance. She went on up the stairs. She opened the door of the room. George was on the bed, reading.

"Did you get the cat?" he asked, putting the book down.

"It was gone."

"Wonder where it went to," he said, resting his eyes from reading.

She sat down on the bed.

"I wanted it so much," she said. "I don't know why I wanted it so much. I wanted that poor kitty. It isn't any fun to be a poor kitty out in the rain."

George was reading again.

She went over and sat in front of the mirror of the dressing table looking at herself with the hand glass. She studied her profile, first one side and then the other. Then she studied the back of her head and her neck.

"Don't you think it would be a good idea if I let my hair grow

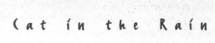

Cat in the Rain

out?" she asked, looking at her profile again.

George looked up and saw the back of her neck, clipped close like a boy's.

"I like it the way it is."

"I get so tired of it," she said. "I get so tired of looking like a boy."

George shifted his position in the bed. He hadn't looked away from her since she started to speak.

"You look pretty darn nice," he said.

She laid the mirror down on the dresser and went over to the window and looked out. It was getting dark.

"I want to pull my hair back tight and smooth and make a big knot at the back that I can feel," she said. "I want to have a kitty to sit on my lap and purr when I stroke her."

"Yeah?" George said from the bed.

"And I want to eat at a table with my own silver and I want candles. And I want it to be spring and I want to brush my hair out in front of a mirror and I want a kitty and I want some new clothes."

"Oh, shut up and get something to read," George said. He was reading again.

His wife was looking out of the window. It was quite dark now and still raining in the palm trees.

"Anyway, I want a cat," she said, "I want a cat. I want a cat now. If I can't have long hair or any fun, I can have a cat."

George was not listening. He was reading his book. His wife looked out of the window where the light had come on in the square.

Someone knocked at the door.

"Avanti," George said. He looked up from his book.

In the doorway stood the maid. She held a big tortoise-shell cat pressed tight against her and swung down against her body.

"Excuse me," she said, "the padrone asked me to bring this for the Signora."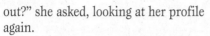

217

My cat and i

by Roger McGough

Girls are simply the prettiest things
My cat and i believe
And we're always saddened
When it's time for them to leave

We watch them titivating
(that often takes a while)
And though they keep us waiting
My cat & i just smile

We like to see them to the door
Say how sad it couldn't last
Then my cat and I go back inside
And talk about the past.

Brushing Your Cat

For regular grooming, nothing beats the standard red rubber two-sided brush available at pet supply stores. To rid a shedding cat of a lot of excess hair, dampen the brush slightly and shake off any excess water before grooming. This brush picks up hair off the furniture, too, and even helps with allergen control, because hair and dander stick to the damp rubber very well. (While you're grooming, be sure to soak off any eye debris with a saline solution or warm water.)

Though a cat doesn't need frequent baths, regular brushing will reduce the amount of fur he ingests and therefore hacks up on your favorite Persian rug. It is especially important to groom long-haired and elderly cats often to prevent mats. Left unattended, matted fur results in pain and skin infections due to constant tugging. Establish a routine while the cat is young.

Does your cat refuse to tolerate brushing? We recommend using grooming mitts, which feels to the cat more like a massage. Put on the mitts or gloves and run your hands all over the cat's body, around his ears, and under his belly. That way, you can check for any mats that will need tending to by a groomer.

Easy Toys for Kitty

Your cat doesn't care whether you spend a lot of money on toys. The key to capturing a cat's interest is a toy that is light in weight. Heavy toys such as the rubber Kongs used for dog play don't work with cats. Beadbags are lighter than beanbags.

Beadbag
strong cotton flannel, chamois, or felt (4" x 8" or smaller); needle and thread (or sewing machine); lightweight hollow plastic beads from a hobby supply store

1. Fold the fabric in half the short way and stitch, using fine stitches or a fine setting on your sewing machine, around three edges, leaving a 1-inch opening. Make sure the stitching is secure enough that the cat can't pull out any thread.

2. Turn the bag right-side out and fill it with beads. Don't overfill or make it heavy. For added intrigue, put in a piece of crinkly cellophane.

3. Sew the opening tightly shut, and toss! Cats like the feel of the extra-soft fabric.

Kitty Kong
toilet paper roll, a small amount of peanut butter

1. If your cat isn't crazy about peanut butter, you can substitute processed cheese food, like Cheez Whiz. Smear a small amount of peanut butter or cheese inside the toilet paper tube (don't overdo it)—just enough so that your pet can smell it or get a tiny taste.

2. Toss the tube and watch the action!

Clicker Training Step 4
Luring

Expert clicker trainers don't like it when an animal trainer leads a pet through a series of performances with a piece of food in front of his face—that's not really training, after all. Nevertheless, a little luring—leading the cat by dangling a desired object in front of him—can be helpful at the very beginning, when you just need to get the behavior. Hurdling, a great exercise for a flabby tabby, can be taught in no time, and is extremely self-reinforcing (fun).

Hurdling
yardstick, broom, or dowel; two stacks of books;
chopstick (optional); clicker; treats

1. Set this up for success, meaning that you erect the hurdle in a hallway or bathroom so that Kitty can't walk around it, and make it low enough so she doesn't limbo. Place a yardstick, broom, or dowel on two stacks of books.
2. Simply make a motion with the chopstick or your hand and say "Over." The cat may step over the stick at first—that's okay.
3. CT (click and treat) the moment all four feet touch the floor on the other side.

Sit Pretty
clicker, treats, chopstick (optional)

1. Invite the cat to sit. CT (click and treat).
2. Ask your cat to sit up by wiggling your fingers above and in front of her head; lure with a treat if you can't get her up. Alternatively, if she is good with the Touch, you can lure with the chopstick.
3. With the other hand, click as she is reaching the top of her ascent, and before she bats at you. Try not to click as she is on her way down, or you will be teaching her to bob. The food lure may be necessary to teach her to start holding the position. (Don't try to make her hold it too long.) Keep CT'ing those reps!
4. Once she starts to get it, add the cue, "Sit pretty."

CAT TALES

Once upon a time there was a fierce and courageous samurai, who was an expert with weapons. His skill with the sword was known throughout the land, and people said that no man or woman could defeat him.

One afternoon as the samurai was placing a bit of fish on the table for his meal, a rat crept stealthily from behind the counter and snatched it away. The samurai saw only its long, oily tail as it dashed into its hiding place.

"Why should I, the greatest samurai in the land, have to share my house with such filthy vermin?" he asked himself. The samurai resolved to rid his house of the rat by any means possible. And so his battle began.

On the first day of battle, the samurai hid himself in a corner and waited for the rat. When he saw his enemy at last, the samurai

The Samurai's Dilemma

A Japanese Folktale

sprang at the furry menace with sword upraised, but the rat moved like lightning and was back to his hole before the sword was even brought down.

Next, the samurai baited traps with delicious morsels and waited for the rat to fall for his trick, but again the wily rat managed to avoid the traps and succeeded in stealing the samurai's dinner. With only a few morsels left on the table, the samurai went to bed hungry for a second night.

On the second day, the samurai comforted himself saying, "I am a very rich man thanks to my many battles. I shall easily buy more food later, but first I must finish this pest," and with that he descended into the village.

At the local dojo, where young warriors practiced their arts, the samurai humbled himself and asked for the help of the master.

"I am looking for a warrior so strong and brave, the rat will have no chance of escape," he declared.

"Look no further," the master, said, motioning to a large tabby. His left ear was half-bitten off and he had a long scar over one of his

eyes. "This cat has fought many battles, and he will live to fight many more!"

The samurai was pleased with such an experienced cat and immediately took him back to the house.

As soon as the rat saw the tabby, he stood absolutely still and stared at the feline warrior. The cat glared back, with a piercing gaze that would set paper aflame. The face-off continued for several breathless moments until, to the samurai's amazement, the cat suddenly dropped his eyes in defeat and ran from the house!

The samurai knew then that this was no ordinary rat. He grabbed his sack of coins to throw at the rat, only to discover that it was surprisingly light. Upon further inspection, the samurai found the rat had chewed a whole in the pouch and stolen the coins!

The samurai went to sleep, hungry and poor.

On the third day, the samurai comforted himself saying, "I am a man with many beautiful things. I shall easily sell my silks and art for money, but first I must finish this pest," and with that he descended into the village.

He went to the local wise man and explained his problem.

"I know a magical cat so swift that she appears like a shadow and

CAT TALES

attacks like smoke. The rat will never even see his enemy until he is clenched between her jaws!" the wise man explained, as he showed the samurai a cat that was black as night. When the cat closed her eyes, she seemed to disappear altogether!

"This will do nicely," the samurai agreed, and took the magical cat to meet her adversary.

As soon as the cat entered the house, she shut her eyes and dissolved into the shadows deep in the corner of the room. The rat, appearing oblivious, meandered out to nibble on the last piece of fruit the samurai had.

Suddenly, the cat materialized and leapt for the rat—only to grab empty space! The rat had deftly jumped from the table before the cat could land. Like quicksilver, the rat swiftly turned and bit his opponent's tail.

The cat let out a piercing yowl and ran from the samurai's house, never to return.

CAT TALES

"Oh you evil, vexing creature!" the samurai shouted at the rat. "You have taken my food, my riches. . ."

Just then, the samurai saw his best silk robe lying on the floor, chewed to threads. He collapsed next to it, devastated. As he looked around his destroyed home, the samurai picked up the half-eaten piece of fruit, wrapped his tattered robe around him, and left his home.

He walked to a nearby temple and sat inside to rest. It was there that he saw a large mother cat with calico fur and green eyes, lazily sunning herself in the courtyard.

"How I wish I was untroubled as that simple cat," the samurai mused aloud.

"She has been with us for many, many years," came a response from behind him. The samurai turned to see a thin monk walking towards him. "In her youth, she was the best mouse catcher for miles around."

"That cat?" the samurai snorted, "She doesn't look like much of a fighter."

"One does not always need to fight to defeat an enemy," the monk replied.

Although the samurai doubted that the cat would be successful against the seemingly invincible pest, he was desperate and begged the monk to lend the calico to him.

CAT TALES

Upon returning to his house with the cat, the samurai was infuriated to see how the rat had destroyed his precious books and paintings.

"That's it, rat!" he exclaimed. But when he put the cat down, she merely yawned, looked around, and then settled into the sunniest part of the room. The samurai looked at his house in shambles, threw up his hands, and retired to his bedroom in defeat. It seemed that the rat was victorious.

For the next few days, the cat did little else but snooze on one of the samurai's prayer cushions. The rat now had the run of the household, and grew bolder with each passing moment. No place was safe from his sharp teeth and scurrying feet, and because the cat put up no opposition, the rat began to feel he was recognized as the superior in the household.

"That cat is little more than a servant to me," thought the rat haughtily as he passed her to retrieve a large piece of bread.

The bread was so heavy, that the rat decided he shouldn't have to deal with carrying it on his own.

"Hey, Puss," he called, "get over here and help me with this!"

The cat opened her eyes, got up, and stretched slowly. She walked over to the bread and placed one paw on it, and then clamped the other swiftly over the rat!

The rat thrashed and fought as hard as he could, but he realized that he was now at the mercy of the cat. Finally, he shrieked, "You have won! Let me go, and I promise never to bother this household again!" And when the cat released him, the rat ran from the house, never to return.

The cat calmly cleaned her fur as the samurai shouted with joy! He thanked the monk a thousand times and gave the temple the rest of his treasured belongings as gifts for the cat's assistance. In return, the monk allowed the samurai to keep the calico in his home.

The clever cat lived with the samurai for many years, and they were never bothered by a rat again. In the end, not only did she become his favorite companion, but she also served as a reminder to him of the lesson that the best way to win a battle is not to fight at all.

You get a wife, you get a house,
Eventually you get a mouse.
You get some words regarding mice,
You get a kitty in a trice.
By two A.M. or thereabout,
The mouse is in, the cat is out.
It dawns upon you, in your cot,
The mouse is silent, the cat is not.
Instead of Pussy, says your spouse,
You should have bought
        another mouse.

The Cat

by Ogden Nash

CAT DANCER This famous interactive toy is tops—any cat with a pulse will work himself into a frenzy over it. Invented in the mid-1990s, its low-tech combo of spring steel and rolled-up cardboard mimics the noise and movement of a fluttering bird.

BEADED MOUSE Offered by the hundreds in pet supply bins, this ubiquitous furry treasure is the best dollar or two ever spent.

BUG JAR They can bat 'em, but they can't catch 'em. This toy, by Happy Dog Toys, safely entertains your cat and even glows in the dark for nocturnal play. "Bugs" float on air currents inside a self-righting jar with a weighted bottom for easy swat and wobble.

Top Toys for Tabby

CRINKLE SACK This is a surefire antidote to boredom. You can make your own crinkler from a paper bag, and punch up the action with tissue paper inside. For added "attack interest," tear a hole at the bottom to poke your finger through, but be careful!

LASER PEN Are you a couch potato, or just too tired to play when you come home from work? A vet recommended a laser pen as an excellent "sit still" way to exercise an active puss. Cats never seem to tire of chasing the light, and no, contrary to rumors, the laser is not strong enough to hurt their eyes.

KITTEN MITTEN There are many variations on the market that promote "wrassling" with your pet while protecting your skin from teeth and claws. Alternatively, you can make your own "cat wrassler" from an oven mitt with a pinch of catnip inside. The mitten is especially good for teething kittens who need to chew.

CATS WITH ATTITUDE PLUSH TOY This safe toy (no parts to swallow or hurt) from Drs. Foster & Smith has a Velcro-closed refillable catnip compartment, for felines who love the herb.

FOAM BALLS AND PING-PONG BALLS A must-have, the lightweight, inexpensive foam balls are available in bags of four or more. Soft enough to pick up with teeth, these are enticing because they roll *and* bounce, and they don't hurt when they hit kitty. Ping-Pong balls are downright addictive.

PANIC MOUSE Many cat owners swear by this expensive motorized toy. It can be set for up to two hours of playtime, and test cats played with it for an average of over an hour.

PEEK-A-PRIZE TOY BOX By SmartCat, this is another solo toy that not only entertains but mentally stimulates your cat as she tries to fish out toys from inside the box. You can make a similar model at home (see Kitty Foosball, p. 70).

Kittens believe that all nature is occupied with their diversion.

—AUGUSTIN-PARADIS DE MONCRIF

D. Merlin

Kibble Dribble

Playing games brings you and your cat closer together. You'll be impressed by your cat's intelligence and his desire to please you (after all, you are his food source!) once he realizes that you want to interact with him on his terms. Kibble Dribble is great fun for kids and satisfies a cat's natural urge to catch and play with prey—just the ticket for a housebound puss who never gets to practice his hunting skills. Most cats use a double-pawed style, but we know one cat who likes to catch and pick up kibble between the toes of one foot. She either eats it out of her paw or sidearms it into the air and chases it!

hard, smooth flooring surface for "bowling" (such as in a kitchen or bathroom), small-size kibble (not treats), a cat ready for action

1. Take up your cat's regular food and water from his feeding area if it's close by.
2. Bowl or bounce a couple of pieces of kibble hard past your cat and watch him try to block. He may even whack them right back at you.
3. If he starts out by eating the kibble right away, keep bowling; he'll catch on, and will spend time "dribbling" it before snacking. Many cats go wild over this, spinning in circles, leaping, and dancing over their "prey."

The Kittens' Quartet

by Carrie Jacobs-Bond

O see, O see the little birds,

  The little birds, the little birds,

O see, O see the little birds,

  All singing in the tree.

All singing in the tree, the tree,

  All singing in the tree;

I suppose they belong to somebody else,

  But I whish they belonged to me.

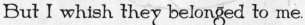

The Cats of Balthus

by Rainer Maria Rilke

Who understands cats? Do you think you do? As far as I'm concerned, their existence has never struck me as more than a fairly risky hypothesis.

If animals are going to belong to our world, they have to come partway into it, agreeing to tolerate to some extent our way of life; if not, whether it's out of hostility or fear, their way of relating will be to measure the distance between us and them.

Think of dogs: their relationship to us is so confidential and full of admiration that some of them seem to have abandoned their most ancient canine traditions to worship our customs and even our mistakes. And that's what makes them tragic and noble. Their decision to let us in forces them to live, so to speak, at the boundaries of their nature, constantly overstepping them with their humanized expressions and sentimental snouts.

But what attitude do cats have?—Cats are cats, and theirs is a cat world from one end to the other. They watch us, you say? But does anyone know if they condescend to hold even for a second our meaningless images at the backs of their eyes? Is their staring simply a kind of opposition, a magic refusal of eyes that have no room for us?–It's true that some of us let ourselves be moved by their cuddly, electrical caress. But they only need to recall how their favorite animal's strange, abrupt loss of attention often put an end to expressions of emotion they thought were reciprocated. And it's those same ones, privileged to be allowed near, who have been denied and rejected many times and, even as they pressed the mysteriously indifferent creature to their bodies, felt themselves stopped at the entrance to that world inhabited exclusively by cats, where they live in the midst of events none of us can even guess at.

Was man ever a contemporary?–I doubt it. And I assure you that sometimes at dusk the neighbor's cat leaps across my path, either unconscious of me or proving to the astonished world of things that I don't even exist.

Do you think I'm wrong to involve you in these reflections, all in the name of leading you up to the story my dear friend Balthus is going to tell you? Granted, he drew it without using words, but by and large his pictures should tell you what you need to know. So why should I repeat them in another form? I'd rather add what has not been said. Let me summarize the story:

Balthus (I think he was ten years old at the time) finds a cat at the Château de Nyon, which you are no doubt familiar with. He is allowed to take him, and off he goes on a trip with his trembling little find. By boat to Geneva, by streetcar to Molard. He introduces his new companion to home life, domesticating, spoiling and treasuring him. "Mitsou" joyfully goes along with the rules and regulations, sometimes breaking the monotony of the house with a playful, ingenious trick. Do you think the fact that his master attaches an annoying leash when he walks him is overdoing it? He does it because he's wary of all the fantasies lurking in the heart of his loving but unknown and adventurous tomcat. However, he's wrong. Even a dangerous move is made without a problem, and the unpredictable little creature adapts to his new surroundings with amused obedience. Then suddenly he disappears. The house is in an uproar; but, thank God, this time it's not serious: they find Mitsou out on the lawn and Balthus, far from scolding the deserter, installs him on the kindly radiator. I guess you can savor, as I do, the rich feeling that follows such anguish. Alas! It's no more than a respite. Sometimes Christmas is too seductive. You eat cake without counting the cost. You get sick, and you go to bed. Mitsou, bothered by your overly long sleep, runs away instead of waking you up. What commotion! Fortunately, Balthus has recovered enough to get right into the search for the runaway. He begins by crawling under his bed: nothing there. Doesn't he look really brave all alone in the cellar with his candle, a symbol of the search that he takes everywhere, into the garden, out in the street: nothing! Look at his solitary little figure: who abandoned him? A cat?—Will his father's recent sketch of Mitsou comfort him? No, there was a sense of foreboding in it, and the loss permanent and inevitable began God only knows when! He comes back inside. He cries, showing you his tears with both hands: Look carefully at them.

That's the whole story. The artist told it better than I could. So what's left for me to say? Very little.

Finding a thing is always fun, because a moment before it didn't exist. But finding a cat: that's incredible! Because, let's admit it, that cat does not enter your life completely as, for example, one plaything or another would. While it's yours now, it's still somewhat apart, and that will always add up to: life + a cat, which, I assure you, is a huge total.

To lose a thing is very sad. You need to imagine it's in poor condition, that wherever it is it's broken or has ended up rotting away. But to lose a cat: No! that's not allowed. No one ever has. How can you lose a cat, a living thing, a live creature, a life? But you can lose a life: that's death!

Right, that's death.

Finding. Losing. Have you considered carefully what loss involves? It's not simply the negation of that generous moment that fulfilled an expectation you yourself weren't aware you had. For between that moment and the loss there is always what we call—awkwardly enough, I admit—possession.

Now loss, as cruel as it is, has no effect on possession. If you like, it ends it or affirms it. But at bottom it's just a second acquisition, this time completely internal, with a different intensity.

And you experienced this, Balthus. No longer seeing Mitsou, you began to see him more.

Is he still alive? He lives on in you who, having delighted in his carefree kittenish gaiety, were obliged to express it through the labors of your sorrow.

And thus, a year later I found you grown and comforted.

But for those who will always see you only at the end of your book, I wrote the first—somewhat fanciful—part of this preface. So I could tell them at the end: "Don't worry: I'm here. So is Balthus. Our world is still intact. There are no cats."

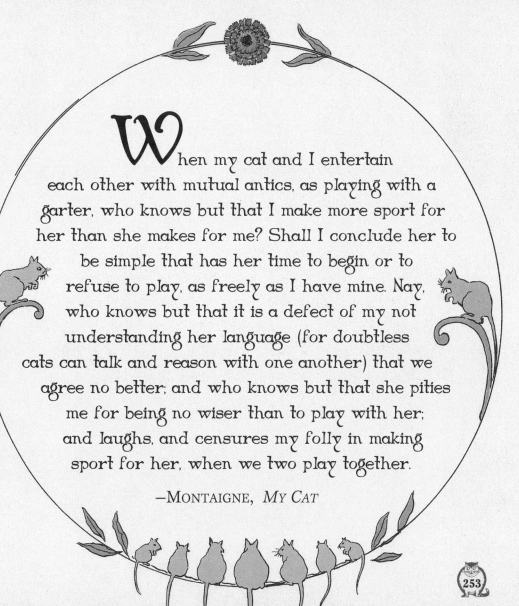

When my cat and I entertain each other with mutual antics, as playing with a garter, who knows but that I make more sport for her than she makes for me? Shall I conclude her to be simple that has her time to begin or to refuse to play, as freely as I have mine. Nay, who knows but that it is a defect of my not understanding her language (for doubtless cats can talk and reason with one another) that we agree no better; and who knows but that she pities me for being no wiser than to play with her; and laughs, and censures my folly in making sport for her, when we two play together.

—MONTAIGNE, *MY CAT*

253

Young Tomcat's Society for Poetic Music

by Heinrich Heine

The Philharmonic Society
Of tomcats met tonight
Upon the roof—but not in heat,
And not to rut or fight.

No summer-night dreams of
    honeymoons,
No serenades will do
In wintertime when snow and ice
Freeze all the gutters through.

A newborn spirit's lately seized
The race of cats—ah, yes,
Young tomcats now are all agog
For Lofty Earnestness.

The old generation's flippancy
Dies out; new aims are rife—
A springtide of cat-poetry
Is stirring in art and life.

The Philharmonic Society
Of tomcats now believe
In artless music—primitive,
Self-sprouting, and naive.

They want poetic music now—
Roulades, not trills that pall,
Poetic instrument and voice—
Which isn't music at all.

They want the reign of genius, though
It may botch things outright,
But in the arts, oft unawares,
It soars to the greatest height.

They honor genius that stays close
To nature as its king,
That does not boast great learning, since
It hasn't learned a thing.

Such *is* the tomcats' program now,
Such are the *aims* they nursed;
And on the roof tonight they had
Their winter concert, the first.

Their *aims* were badly carried out,
Those grandiose views of theirs—
Go hang yourself, dear Berlioz,
For missing such affairs!

It was a loud uproar as if
Three dozen bagpipes played
A brandy-soaked fandango fling
Or a barnyard gallopade,

A jumbled din *as* if the beasts
On Noah's Ark had begun
To serenade the rising flood,
And all *in* unison.

What croaks and bawls and caterwauls,
What bellows of all *sorts!*
The drafty chimneys joined right *in*
With church chorales *in* snorts.

One voice rang clear above them all,
Somehow both shrill and wan,

Just like the voice that Sontag had
By the time her voice was gone.

Wild concert! A great paean sung
In utter impudence
To celebrate the victory
Of madness over sense.

Perhaps they were rehearsing there
An opera to beguile 'em
By Hungary's greatest pianist
For Charenton Asylum.

This witches' sabbath ended when
Day dawned on these domains;
It made a pregnant cook bed down
With premature labor pains.

This poor befuddled woman had
No memory any more;
She did not know the father of
The baby that she bore.

Say, Lisa, was it Peter? Paul?
The father—tell us that!—
She smiles, and beams, and then she says:
"O Liszt, divine tomcat!"

Playtime Safety

When choosing or making a pet toy, behaviorists recommend that you not give anything to your cat that you wouldn't give to a three-year-old. This means no harmful parts, such as glitter, tinsel, buttons, or small, unconcealed jingle bells that could come off and be accidentally swallowed. String, lengths of yarn, thread, fishing line, and rubber bands can be swallowed whole, causing intestinal obstruction. The end of a string can be swallowed while the other end gets caught around kitty's tongue. If you see string, thread, or yarn hanging out of your cat's mouth, do not pull on it; it can cut her internally. Rush her to your veterinarian. Elastic cords and feathers, too, are often chewed through; these toys are meant for supervised, interactive use only, and should be put away when playtime's over. Conversely, say vets, there is no harm done if a healthy cat shreds up and happens to eat some pieces of a paper bag.

Cats often like to hide out in plastic bags, but if they get their head stuck in a handle, they might panic, causing choking or suffocating.

According to the ASPCA, you should never use your hands or fingers as play objects with kittens. This type of rough play may cause biting and scratching behaviors to develop as your kitten matures.

Macaroni Hockey

No, your cat couldn't care less about scoring goals, but this "hockey rink" is sure to produce merriment among furry friends. Cats love to place one object inside another (many a small toy has been found dropped in the water bowl or stuffed inside a shoe), and Macaroni Hockey takes advantage of this kitty behavior. It's also self-reinforcing, in that cats often will play it on their own—that is, until the "puck" ends up under the refrigerator!

2 lightweight plastic storage containers (each about 6″ x 10″ x 2″), duct or package-sealing tape, 2 pieces corrugated cardboard (each about 12″ x 14″), uncooked large-size pasta, a playful puss

1. Tape each plastic container on its long side to the end of each piece of cardboard. The opening should align the edge of the cardboard. Position these "goals" at least 6 feet apart and place heavy books or other weights on the cardboard pieces to hold in place.

2. Shoot a couple of pieces of uncooked pasta into the goal. Your cat will probably join right in. Don't expect her to make a lot of goals, but she'll love the clattering sound the pasta makes when she scores! Because it's so lightweight for its size, cats also love to pick up and carry pasta, so you will have to make allowances for "infractions" like traveling with puck in mouth. Some cats even like to carry it to the goal.

Clicker Training Step 5
Shaping

You've already tried a little shaping—modifying a behavior in tiny increments—with the Gimme Ten. Zen Kitty is for the clicker-wise cat who has learned the Gimme Five (page 163), and will test your pet's understanding of the clicker game.

Cats *adore* Pick It Up—especially kittens, who love to put things in their mouths. It's also a challenging way to learn more about how to shape behaviors.

As you continue to practice for a few minutes every day, your cat will begin to offer desirable behaviors more frequently, and will spend less time on destructive projects. After she learns this trick, she may start bringing you all manner of items from around the house.

clicker, treats, and props as required below

Pick It Up

1. Place a lightweight toy or foam ball, reserved for training only, in front of the cat. CT as you see the jaw start to move. Wiggle it around if he doesn't bite it.
2. "Accidentally" bump it into his mouth. CT! If the jaw starts

to open, click fast, and treat. Repeat. CT for contact, biting, and finally pickups, and add the verbal cue, "Pick it up."

Zen Kitty

1. This is for the clicker-wise cat who has learned the Gimme Five. Present him with two fists: one empty, one with a treat inside. He will have a tendency to go for the one with the treat, but wiggle the empty one. If he gets so frustrated he walks away, try withdrawing the hand with the treat and simply CT'ing him a few times for patting an empty fist.
2. Start over with the two fists. As soon as he pats the empty fist, CT, open the other hand, and let him retrieve the delicious treasure inside. Repeat the Zen experience.

The White and Black Dynasties

by Théophile Gautier

– i –

To gain the friendship of a cat is not an easy thing. It is a philosophic, well-regulated, tranquil animal, a creature of habit and a lover of order and cleanliness. It does not give its affections indiscriminately. It will consent to be your friend if you are worthy of the honor, but it will not be your slave. With all its affection, it preserves its freedom of judgment, and it will not do anything for you which it considers unreasonable; but once it has given its love, what absolute confidence, what fidelity of affection! It will make itself the companion of your hours of work, of loneliness, or of sadness. It will lie the whole evening on your knee, purring and happy in your society, and leaving the company of creatures of its own kind to be with you. In vain the sound of caterwauling reverberates from the house-tops, inviting it to one of those cats' evening parties where essence of red-herring takes the place of tea. It will not be tempted, but continues to keep its vigil with you. If you put it down it climbs up again quickly, with a sort of crooning noise, which is like a gentle reproach. Sometimes, when seated in front of you, it gazes at you with such soft, melting eyes, such a human and caressing look, that you are almost awed, for it seems impossible that reason can be absent from it.

– i i –

I called her Seraphita, in memory of Balzac's Swedenborgian

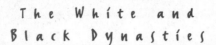

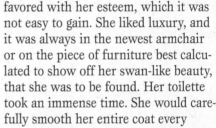

romance. The heroine of that wonderful story, when she climbed the snow peaks of the Falberg with Minna, never shone with a more pure white radiance. Seraphita had a dreamy and pensive character. She would lie motionless on a cushion for hours, not asleep, but with eyes fixed in rapt attention on

scenes invisible to ordinary mortals. Caresses were agreeable to her, but she responded to them with great reserve, and only to those of people whom she favored with her esteem, which it was not easy to gain. She liked luxury, and it was always in the newest armchair or on the piece of furniture best calculated to show off her swan-like beauty, that she was to be found. Her toilette took an immense time. She would carefully smooth her entire coat every morning, and wash her face with her paw, and every hair on her body shone like new silver when brushed by her pink tongue. If anyone touched her she would immediately efface all traces of the contact, for she could not endure being ruffled. Her elegance and distinction gave one an idea of aristocratic birth, and among her own kind she must have been at least a duchess. She had a passion for scents. She would plunge her

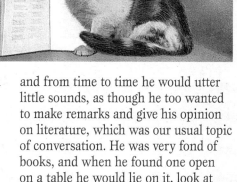

nose into bouquets, and nibble a perfumed handkerchief with little paroxysms of delight. She would walk about on the dressing-table sniffling the stoppers of the scent-bottles, and she would have loved to use the violet powder if she had been allowed.

Such was Seraphita, and never was a cat more worthy of a poetic name.

— i i i —

Don Pierrot, like all animals which are spoilt and made much of, developed a charming amiability of character. He shared the life of the household with all the pleasure which cats find in the intimacy of the domestic hearth. Seated in his usual place near the fire, he really appeared to understand what was being said, and to take an interest in it. His eyes followed the speakers, and from time to time he would utter little sounds, as though he too wanted to make remarks and give his opinion on literature, which was our usual topic of conversation. He was very fond of books, and when he found one open on a table he would lie on it, look at the page attentively, and turn over the leaves with his paw; then he would end by going to sleep, for all the world as if he were reading a fashionable novel.

Directly I took up a pen he would jump on my writing-desk and with deep attention watch the steel nib tracing black spider-

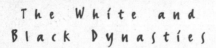

legs on the expanse of white paper, and his head would turn each time I began a new line. Sometimes he tried to take part in the work, and would attempt to pull the pen out of my hand, no doubt in order to write himself, for he was an aesthetic cat, like Hoffman's Murr, and I strongly suspect him of having scribbled his memoirs at night on some house-top by the light of his phosphorescent eyes. Unfortunately these lucubrations have been lost.

Don Pierrot never went to bed until I came in. He waited for me inside the door, and as I entered the hall he would rub himself against my legs and arch his back, purring joyfully all the time. Then he proceeded to walk in front of me like a page, and if I had asked him, he would certainly have carried the candle for me. In this fashion he escorted me to my room and waited while I undressed; then he would jump on the bed, put his paws round my neck, rub noses with me, and lick me with his rasping little pink tongue, while giving vent to soft inarticulate cries, which clearly expressed how pleased he was to see me again. Then when his transports of affection had subsided, and the hour for repose had come, he would balance himself on the rail of the bedstead and sleep there like a bird perched on a bough. When I woke in the morning he would come and lie near me until it was time to get up. Twelve o'clock was the hour at

which I was supposed to come in. On this subject Pierrot had all the notions of a concierge.

At that time we had instituted little evening gatherings among a few friends, and had formed a small society, which we called the Four Candles Club, the room in which we met being, as it happened, lit by four candles in silver candlesticks, which were placed at the corners of the table.

Sometimes the conversation became so lively that I forgot the time, at the risk of finding, like Cinderella, my carriage turned into a pumpkin and my coachman into a rat.

Pierrot waited for me several times until two o'clock in the morning, but in the end my conduct displeased him, and he went to bed without me. This mute protest against my innocent dissipation touched me so much that ever after I came home regularly at midnight. But it was a long time before Pierrot forgave me. He wanted to be sure that it was not a sham repentance; but when he was convinced of the sincerity of my conversion, he deigned to take me into favor again, and he resumed his nightly post in the entrance-hall.

— i v —

Enjolras was by far the handsomest of his family. He was remarkable for his great leonine head and big ruff, his powerful shoulders, long back and splendid feathery tail. There was something theatrical about him, and he seemed to be always posing like a popular actor who knows he is being admired. His movements were slow, undulating and majestic. He put each foot down with as much circumspection as if he were walking on a table covered with Chinese bric-à-brac or Venetian glass. As to his character, he was by no means a stoic, and he showed a love of eating which that virtuous and sober

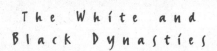

young man, his namesake, would certainly have disapproved. Enjolras would undoubtedly have said to him, like the angel to Swedenborg: "You eat too much."

I humored this gluttony, which was as amusing as a gastronomic monkey's, and Enjolras attained a size and weight seldom reached by the domestic cat. It occurred to me to have him shaved poodle-fashion, so as to give the finishing touch to his resemblance to a lion.

We left him his mane and a big tuft at the end of his tail, and I would not swear that we did not give him mutton-chop whiskers on his haunches like those Munito wore. Thus tricked out, it must be confessed he was much more like a Japanese monster than an African lion. Never was a more fantastic whim carved out of a living animal.

His shaven skin took odd blue tints, which contrasted strangely with his black mane.

— v —

The cat named after the interesting Eponine was more delicate and slender than her brothers. Her nose was rather long, and her eyes slightly oblique, and green as those of Pallas Athene, to whom Homer always applied the epithet of γλαυχωπιϛ. Her nose was of velvety black, with the grain of a fine Périgord truffle; her whiskers were in a perpetual state of agitation, all of which gave her a peculiarly expressive countenance. Her superb black coat was always in motion, and was watered and shot with shadowy markings. Never was there a more sensitive, nervous, electric animal. If one stroked her two or three times in the dark, blue sparks would fly crackling out of her fur.

Eponine attached herself particularly to me, like the Eponine of the novel to Marius, but I, being less taken up with Cosette than that handsome young man, could

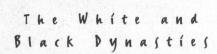

accept the affection of this gentle and devoted cat, who still shares the pleasure of my suburban retreat and is the inseparable companion of my hours of work.

She comes running up when she hears the front-door bell, receives the visitors, conducts them to the drawing-room, talks to them—yes, talks to them—with little chirruping sounds, that do not in the least resemble the language cats use in talking to their own kind, but which simulate the articulate speech of man. What does she say? She says in the clearest way, "Will you be good enough to wait till monsieur comes down? Please look at the pictures, or chat with me in the meantime, if that will amuse you." Then when I come in she discreetly retires to an armchair or a corner of the piano, like a well-bred animal who knows what is correct in good society. Pretty little Eponine gave so many proofs of intelligence, good disposition and sociability, that by common consent she was raised to the dignity of a *person*, for it was quite evident that she was possessed of higher reasoning power than mere instinct. This dignity conferred on her the privilege of eating at table like a person instead of out of a saucer in a corner of the room like an animal.

So Eponine had a chair next to me at breakfast and dinner, but on account of her small size she was allowed to rest her two front paws on the edge of the table. Her place was laid, without spoon or fork, but she had her glass. She went right through dinner dish by dish, from soup to dessert, waiting for her turn to be helped, and behaving with

such propriety and nice manners as one would like to see in many children. She made her appearance at the first sound of the bell, and on going into the dining-room one found her already in her place, sitting up in her chair with her paws resting on the edge of the table-cloth, and seeming to offer you her little face to kiss, like a well-brought-up little girl who is affectionately polite towards her parents and elders.

As one finds flaws in diamonds, spots on the sun, and shadows on perfection itself, so Eponine, it must be confessed, had a passion for fish. She shared this in common with all other cats. Contrary to the Latin proverb,

> *"Catus amat pisces, sed non*
> *vult tingere plantas,"*

she would willingly have dipped her paw into the water if by so doing she could have pulled out a trout or a young carp. She became nearly frantic over fish, and, like a child who is filled with the expectation of dessert, she sometimes rebelled at her soup when she knew (from previous investigations in the kitchen) that fish was coming. When this happened she was not helped, and I would say to her coldly: "Mademoiselle, a person who is not hungry for soup cannot be hungry for fish," and the dish would be pitilessly carried away from under her nose. Convinced that matters were serious, greedy Eponine would swallow her soup in all haste, down to the last drop, polishing off the last crumb of bread or bit of macaroni, and would then turn round and look at me with pride, like someone who has conscientiously done his duty. She was then given her portion, which she consumed with great satisfaction, and after tasting of every dish in turn, she would finish up by drinking a third of a glass of water.

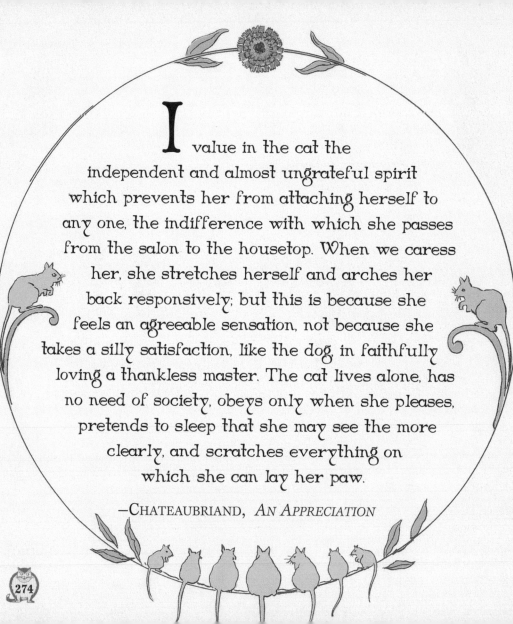

I value in the cat the independent and almost ungrateful spirit which prevents her from attaching herself to any one, the indifference with which she passes from the salon to the housetop. When we caress her, she stretches herself and arches her back responsively; but this is because she feels an agreeable sensation, not because she takes a silly satisfaction, like the dog, in faithfully loving a thankless master. The cat lives alone, has no need of society, obeys only when she pleases, pretends to sleep that she may see the more clearly, and scratches everything on which she can lay her paw.

—CHATEAUBRIAND, *AN APPRECIATION*

The touch of a hand is warm, soothing, and relaxing. Working animals such as police and assistance dogs, performing animals, and therapy pets, who are subjected to daily stresses, often benefit from regular therapeutic rubdowns. Why not your house cat, too? Once you have developed a bond with your cat through massage, you may even be able to tell when he isn't feeling well.

TAKE YOUR CUES FROM YOUR CAT Massage therapists who have transferred their knowledge to working with cats say the secret is: Don't massage areas that the cat doesn't want touched. Let your cat advise you of what she likes and doesn't like. Next time your "belly cat" plunges in front of you, take a moment to honor her invitation. Begin at her chest and stroke in little circles, moving lightly downward. When your little sidestroker solicits you by "swimming" toward you on the carpet, think how he might appreciate a deep, gentle shoulder rub with your thumbs. And your "bowing cat" who asks you to "thump her rump" might enjoy a vigorous friction backrub to work the kinks out. Take a few moments to try massage on a regular basis.

USE YOUR HANDS AS GROOMING TOOLS Dampening your palms will allow you to get rid of shed fur that is trapped in the coat and that the cat would ingest through licking. Stroke in all directions with the flats of your hands. Then run through the fur one more time, checking the skin with your fingertips for lesions, ticks, or bites.

Massaging Your Cat

START WITH THE SPINE Work your thumbs and fingers in a circular pattern along the sides of the backbone from neck to tail, never losing touch with the skin. Move to the sides, then along the hips and back legs. Return to the shoulders.

PAY ATTENTION TO FAVORITE AREAS There is no end to the annals of weird things cats like—we even read of a cat who begged to have the roof of his mouth massaged! The side of the jaw between ear and chin is a definite yes: You may have noticed your cat forcefully rubbing everything within reach with the scent glands in her cheeks (marking). Expect intense purring.

EXPLORE NEW TERRITORY Think of a cat's ears the way humans think of their feet. We don't like it when they're tickled, and that's why foot doctors know to touch them firmly. Gently massage the back edge of your cat's ears between your thumbs and forefingers, using a circular, almost tugging motion at the tips. Some swear that this puts cats into a hypnotic state—but if your furry pal doesn't like it, don't force it! Keep returning to your pet's favorite spots between new territories. Stroking along the backs of the hind legs, if the cat tolerates it, triggers a reflex that looks as if the cat is doing the splits.

PLAY "THIS LITTLE PIGGY" Try massaging your cat's foot pads, tugging gently on her toes while she's relaxed and lying on her side. She likes it if she spreads her feet and extends her legs toward you, or, if lying on her back, she "pedals" an imaginary bicycle.

Keep It Fresh!

There's a reason why motorized toys have timers, and crinkle sacks turn into "nap sacks." Left on or out all the time, toys and other props simply become part of the background. Because cats have evolved as efficient hunting machines, their perception is based on movement and novelty in the environment. Preserve that novelty by putting toys on rotation, using a toy chest or basket for playthings that are currently on sabbatical. You might even place the basket in different spots where Puss can happen upon it and joyfully rifle through it. Keep catnip and catnip toys in a drawer, though—you don't want a total "herbhead!" Do likewise with toys that require supervision.

What's happening when
you hear "woof ... *splat* ...
meow ... *splat*"?
> *It's raining cats and dogs.*

Did you hear about the cat
who drank five bowls of water?
> *He set a new lap record.*

What do you get when you
cross a chick with an alley cat?
> *A peeping tom.*

What's the difference between
a cat and a comma?
> *One has the paws before the claws
> and the other has the clause
> before the pause.*

What is a cat's way of keeping
law and order?
> *Claw Enforcement.*

What is a cat's favorite colour?
> *Purrrrrrrple!*

Feline Funnies

How did a cat take first
prize at the bird show?
*She just jumped up to the cage,
reached in, and took it.*

What happened when the
cat went to the flea circus?
He stole the whole show!

What do you call a cat that
has swallowed a duck?
A duck-filled fatty puss.

Why is the cat so grouchy?
Because she's in a bad mewd.

What do cats like to eat
for breakfast?
Mice Krispies.

How do cats end a fight?
They hiss and make up.

Why did the cat put oil on
the mouse? *Because it squeaked.*

The Cat Who Came for Christmas

by Cleveland Amory

Cats . . . like routine—in fact they love it. And, in the days—and nights—which followed the rescue my cat and I worked out many routines. Or rather he worked them out, and I, as dutifully as I could, worked at following them.

Some of these routines necessarily involved compromises. My cat, for example, liked to get up early—in fact he liked to get up at 3 A.M. That was, of course, all right with me. His hours, it had been one of our understandings, were his own. The trouble was that, at 3 A.M., he liked a midnight snack of Tender Vittles. Again, seemingly, no problem. Simply leave out a bowl of Vittles before he went to bed.

But unfortunately there was a problem. I could not just leave out a bowl of Vittles before I went to bed. He would eat them before he went to bed. He did not have, when you came right down to it, either any good old-fashioned Boston discipline—as I would have thought he would have at least begun to learn from me—or, for that matter, my good sound sensible Boston foresight. No matter how large a bowl I filled of Vittles before he retired, the bowl was empty before he retired.

His hours in this routine thus became my hours. And so we compromised. Before going to bed each night, I put out an empty dish on the floor by the bed and a package of Tender vittles on my bedside table. At 3 a.m.—and he was extraordinarily accurate about this—he would wake up, roll over, and wake me up. At 3:01 I would roll over, put some Vittles in his dish, or at least reasonably near it, and go back, or at least attempt to go back, to sleep.

In the real morning we had to have another compromise. This one was about water.

My cat did not actively dislike all water. He just disliked vertical water—as in rain or shower baths. He did not mind it coming down in small quantities as out of a faucet—in fact he was very fond of it that way. But it had to be small quantities. If it was to be in large quantities, then he firmly insisted on his water being horizontal. This he was especially fond of when I was in it—as in a regular tub bath. He did not like the shower at any time, whether I was in it or not.

So, again, we compromised. Although I had always taken showers, I gave up showers and took tubs instead. Baths, I decided, really get you much cleaner than showers do anyway. Also, whether this was true or not, I very much liked the additional routine which he had developed, and which I had followed, which went with the bath. What he would do, once I was in the tub, was to jump up on the edge of the tub—a precarious leap, considering his game hip—balance himself, and then make a slow solemn trip around. He would start first toward the back of the tub, stopping at each point when he got to my shoulders. Here he would lean toward me, give me a head nudge and a small nip, and then proceed on. When he got to the business end of the tub, he would carefully investigate the spout, and, if I had not turned it on just enough for him to drink a few drops, he would turn and tell me to do so. And, of course, I would.

. . . I want to make clear that my cat and I did not have, by any stretch of the imagination, your normal morning repast. Indeed, perhaps the most remarkable of all the routines which we developed was here involved. For the plain fact of the matter is that, before its development anywhere else, and long before its adoption by the upper echelons of big business, my cat and I pioneered, all by ourselves, the power breakfast.

This too began with a compromise. My cat was very fond of breakfast, and, after he had eaten his, he was very fond of

eating mine too. In vain I remonstrated with him that he
was being selfish and inconsiderate. In vain also I lectured
him that I had been brought up in a home where animals
were not allowed in the dining room at any time, even
when no meals were being served. As for his habit, without
so much as a buy my leave, of getting up on the table and
taking a bite here and a bite there, of anything he pleased,
from cereal to eggs or whatever, it would have to stop. It
simply could not or would not be tolerated by me, and that
was that.

So, once more, we compromised. I agreed to let him up on
the table if no other guests were present, and he in turn
agreed not to eat anything at the same time I was eating it.
The gray area in this compromise was the question of when
I had my spoon or fork in my mouth, and he was not sure
whether or not it was going back to where it came from or
was finished: whose turn, then, was it—his or mine?
Eventually we worked this out—if the spoon was still in
motion, it was still my turn; if it wasn't, it was his.

All in all, it was a power breakfast all right, and a great
deal was accomplished. For one thing, when I was late
and/or he was particularly hungry, I am sure we several
times broke the standing Guinness record, and possibly the
Olympic as well, for a single breakfast totally consumed by
two partners.

Finicky or Fat?

Make sure your finicky cat is hungry at mealtimes: Two or three meals a day is fine. Put the food out and give a picky cat some time—up to about six hours if you can stand the temper tantrums—before giving in and trying something different. A cat who does not eat for 24 hours, however, should be taken to the vet.

FINICKY FELINES Many a tale is told of the finicky feline. Frustrated humans owned by picky kitties often feel forced to lay out a smorgasbord that includes salmon, chicken, turkey, whitefish, lamb, veal, herring, and more. The turning up of the feline nose, however, usually stems less from a cat's haughty nature and more from feeding routines that offer too much food between meals. Your vet may recommend gradually cutting back on free-feeding. To avoid stomach upset, it's also advisable not to feed a huge variety of proteins or to constantly change from one food or flavor to another. Sometimes a treat can jump-start a finicky cat's appetite and get him heading for the food bowl. Try some of the tempting treats in this book to rev up your furry monsters.

FAT CATS One way to determine if your cat is overweight is through massage. Gently run your hands around your cat's rib cage and see how easily you can feel the bones beneath the skin. If you can't feel the ribs at all, your cat is too chubby. Dieting can be tricky in cats, so *consult your vet before putting your cat on a diet.* Free-feeding of high-carbohydrate dry food is often the culprit. One thing you can do is to increase his calorie expenditure. Find a toy your cat is willing to interact with and play with him more often.

Clicker Training
Practical Clicking*

Get Off the Counter!

The method that trainers employ to replace undesirable behaviors is called *training an incompatible behavior.*

Your cat probably gets on the counter because she gets attention for it—even negative attention. Place a fairly high chair or stool near the counter. At first, click and treat the cat whenever she jumps to the chair. Clicking with your mouth is fine. She will soon realize that being on the counter gets her nothing, but jumping to the chair earns rewards. Sitting on the chair is incompatible with counter surfing. After a while, stop treating her each time. The behavior will only get stronger as she tries to get your attention in the way she's now conditioned. Give her food or affection every so often. This is called a *variable interval of reinforcement*, and is one of the most effective tools of operant conditioning.

In the event your little surfer gets up to mischief while you are out, you can use *aversives*. Cover the counter with foil and sprinkle it with water (cats don't like walking on foil). Line the edge of the counter with cans filled with just enough pennies to

Practical Clicking

make noise—not too heavy to be knocked off (don't test this in front of the cat). The foil and the loud noise of the penny cans will make that counter an unpleasant place to be. You should have to do this for only about a week. Combine this method with the chair solution above. Oh, and make sure you don't store your cat's food on or near the counter.

*Assumes your cat is clicker-wise.

Practical Clicking

Clipping Claws

Teach your cat the Gimme Five (page 163). Make sure he is doing it consistently. When he lays his paw in your hand, begin by very gently holding it for a fraction of a second longer. CT! Resist the urge the urge to squeeze, grab, or forcibly hold the cat's leg. Over a series of sessions, gradually move to lifting a toe for a second. Do not try to clip—just look at a claw, drop the paw, CT! Some cats take days or a couple of weeks to get to this point. Use baby steps and treats until finally you can zoom in and clip a tiny end off one claw without his fighting you. Jackpot your pet! Now things will get much easier, because he realizes that each clip means a treat. Eventually you will have a cat who presents his paw for a manicure, or at least will allow you to clip without a fight.

Carriers

This is a project for the cat and human with clicker experience. It will probably take three weeks of short daily sessions.

Your cat should know Touch well enough to come to the prop from across a room. Use a Sherpa Bag or similar cat-comfy carrier. Leave the carrier out for a few days. Play Magic Box

Practical Clicking

(page 190) with your cat. Use the prop you used to teach Touch to gradually lead your 'fraidy cat closer (click and treat) and finally into the carrier. Click and treat for putting even one paw into the carrier. You can even put treats just inside the door if it will get her head in there. Do not touch the cat. If she goes inside, do not close the door; click and toss in a treat. You might feed the cat her dinner there, once she gets used to going inside. Eventually you will find her in the carrier, waiting for a treat.

Once she's opting to stay inside the carrier regularly, try closing the door for a second, click and treat. The cat will pop right out at first, and you'll have to back-track. Keep lengthening the time you close the door as she gets used to this activity. If she approves, let her sit for a short time with the carrier closed (poke treats in; if she's not too scared to eat, she's okay). Continue leaving the carrier out and giving rewards at random to strengthen the association with food. Lengthen the time with door closed at each session.

Follow the same baby steps for conditioning your cat to the car!

*Assumes your cat is clicker-wise.

To a Cat

by
John Keats

Cat! who hast pass'd thy grand climacteric,
    How many mice and rats hast in thy days
    Destroy'd? How many tit-bits stolen? Gaze
With those bright languid segments green, and
    prick
Those velvet ears—but prythee do not stick
    Thy latent talons in me—and tell me all thy frays,
Of fish and mice, and rats and tender chick;
Nay, look not down, nor lick thy dainty wrists—
    For all the wheezy asthma—and for all
Thy tail's tip is nick'd off—and though the fists
    Of many a maid have given thee many a maul,
Still is thy fur as when the lists
    In youth thou enter'dst on glass-bottled wall.

Sardine Sandies

Cats' ideas about what constitutes a cookie are very different from our own! If you have more than one cat, expect to find a convention of furry beggars underfoot as you prepare these. Choose whole sardines that have no salt added in processing (you can add your own).

$1/_3$ can sardines, drained, with $1/_2$ teaspoon oil reserved

200 IU vitamin E (from a capsule), as an antioxidant

$1/_3$ cup plain bread crumbs or cracker crumbs

1 egg, beaten

$1/_2$ teaspoon brewer's yeast

dash of salt

1. Preheat the oven to warm or its lowest setting.
2. In a small bowl, mash the sardines very well. Puncture the vitamin E capsule and drizzle it over the fish.
3. Add the remaining ingredients and mix well.
4. Drop tiny portions about the size of the tip of your little finger onto a cookie sheet generously greased with butter or shortening (cats don't have to worry about cholesterol). Do not form into balls; they don't bake well, and cats can't bite into them easily.
5. Dry in the oven for 40 minutes, turning once halfway through. Stored in an airtight container in the fridge, these keep for 4–5 days.

Makes 7–8 dozen.

CAT TALES

There are as many different cats in the world as there are stars in the sky—Fat cats; skinny cats; long-haired and short-haired cats; black, brown, and white cats; and cats with any other color you could imagine. Yet there's one cat that has a very peculiar characteristic: the little Manx has no tail. But that's not the way it always was.

How the Manx Cat Lost His Tail

A Western European Tale

Long ago, back when Noah was first preparing for the Great Flood by building the Ark, the Manx cat had a beautiful, long tail that was the envy of all the other animals. And this is the story of how he lost it.

God told Noah that a flood was about to wash over the world, cleansing it of wickedness and sin, and that the only ones

CAT TALES

deemed worthy enough to save were Noah, his family, and the innocent animals of the world. So Noah set about gathering two of each animal to be loaded up on his Ark. In order to better organize matters, Noah called the animals to him and explained the situation.

"So, we're going on a cruise?" one giraffe asked.

"You could call it that," Noah answered.

"Ooh, I've always wanted to go on one, but never quite found the time!" the other giraffe exclaimed.

Noah cleared his throat, "I've got word that in a week, this planet is going to turn into the world's largest swimming pool, so it's important for us all to all get ready for when that time, okay?"

All the animals nodded and immediately dispersed to prepare for the trip, except for the Manx, who sat licking his tail, lost in thought.

"Manx?" Noah said, but the cat didn't turn. Noah spoke louder, " Manx!" The cat shot up suddenly and looked at Noah.

"This is serious, Manx. Be ready, or I'll have you by that beautiful tail."

Manx nodded and then begin to think, "I've got a whole week. What

should I do with myself for a whole week? Wait a minute! Only a week, then the only mice I'll see for a while will be the two on the Ark. And I won't even be able to touch them!" This thought made him so miserable, that he began hunting as many mice as he could, as fast as he could.

The week quickly passed quickly, and on the last day, ominous storm clouds began rolling in. Noah had finished the Ark and was ready for his first passengers.

"Okay, let's get a move on now," he ordered the animals, as they began to file onto the Ark.

"You're sure we'll be safe on there?" one gazelle asked as he eyed the lions suspiciously.

"Absolutely," replied Noah, "Now step right up, biggest to smallest!"

While the rest of the animals were lining up to board the Ark, the Manx cat was still busy chasing mice. He stopped to notice the other animals waiting to get on the Ark and declared, "Oh, I have plenty of time before it's my turn!" Then he jumped at an unsuspecting rodent.

The hours went by, and fat drops of rain began to fall. Two of each animal were carefully noted and then led onto the ship. By the time they

CAT TALES

303

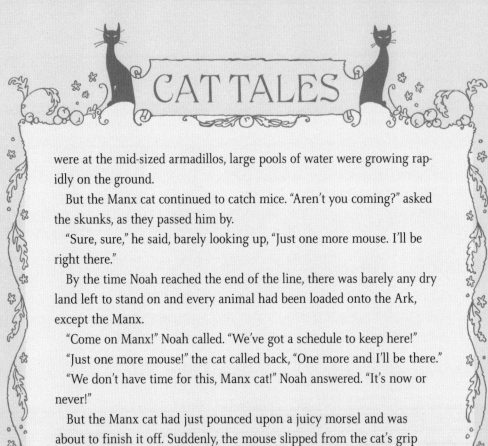

were at the mid-sized armadillos, large pools of water were growing rapidly on the ground.

But the Manx cat continued to catch mice. "Aren't you coming?" asked the skunks, as they passed him by.

"Sure, sure," he said, barely looking up, "Just one more mouse. I'll be right there."

By the time Noah reached the end of the line, there was barely any dry land left to stand on and every animal had been loaded onto the Ark, except the Manx.

"Come on Manx!" Noah called. "We've got a schedule to keep here!"

"Just one more mouse!" the cat called back, "One more and I'll be there."

"We don't have time for this, Manx cat!" Noah answered. "It's now or never!"

But the Manx cat had just pounced upon a juicy morsel and was about to finish it off. Suddenly, the mouse slipped from the cat's grip and bolted.

"Oh bother," he declared, as he chased the scurrying mouse.

Now, luckily for the Manx cat, the mouse was heading directly for

CAT TALES

the Ark door, where at that very moment, they were closing up the ship. Quick as a wink, the mouse darted inside and directly behind him came the Manx cat!

But just as he had pounced on the little mouse inside, he let out an ear-splitting screech, "YOOOWWWW!!"

For you see, although most of the Manx cat was inside the Ark, its poor, beautiful tail had still not made it across the threshold, and before he knew what had happened, the door shut tight. The Manx cat was left with nothing but a sorry looking rump, while his long tail was left outside. He was so distraught that he let go of the little mouse, and wept and yowled over the fate of his poor tail.

The rest of the animals tried to console him, but Noah said, "Serves you right. Let that be a lesson to you! Never let pleasure get in the way of what needs to be done."

And to this day, the Manx cat is a very meek and modest creature. Perhaps because it remembers its luxurious tail lost so long ago.

The Thing
About Cats

by John L'Heureux

Cats hang out with witches quite a lot;
that's not it.

The thing about cats is
they're always looking at you.
Especially when you're asleep.

Some cats pretend they're not looking
until you're not looking.
They are not to be trusted.

Bath Time!

If you need to shampoo your cat, use vet-recommended products like DermaPet's acetic acid/boric acid formula, without soaps or dyes, or Drs. Foster & Smith Oatmeal Shampoo. Many store-bought pet shampoos are for dogs only, and human shampoos are usually too harsh. If you are lucky enough to have an elevated laundry tub, you can fashion a grate for the bottom out of heavy steel window screening. Bend the sharp edges of the grate downward and make sure that it fits in the tub securely. The cat will latch on to the screen with her claws. First, gently pour warm water over your cat's back from a cup—not a sprayer—and lather up. For an uncontrollable beastie, you can place a second screen over the top of the tub and shower her through it. Be careful to keep water and shampoo out of kitty's face. When done, you can lift her up by raising the screen. Bundle her up in warm towels and use a hair dryer on very low if your pet permits. Cats who find baths truly traumatizing should be bathed at the vet's, where they can receive a mild sedative.

> "To bathe a cat takes brute force, perseverance, courage of conviction, and a cat. The last ingredient is usually hardest to come by."
> —STEPHEN BAKER

Stair Bounce

If you find the right big, light, soft fuzzy ball, cats will vote for the Stair Bounce as Best Cat Game, every time. Children, too, can be entertained by Kitty's upstairs-downstairs antics for hours. This game is great for "wearing out" mischeivous kittens who have a penchant for getting into everything. Cats find sheepskin-covered balls particularly irresistible.

lightweight, medium- to large-size fleece or sheepskin-covered ball (around 6-inches maximum) from a pet supply store; a "step-wise" cat

1. Use a lightweight toy that rolls and bounces, and is soft enough for a cat to sink her teeth and claws into. Do not use a sparkle ball or other smooth, heavy ball that the cat can't grab. A sheepskin ball or large, soft foam ball is perfect. If it's catnip-impregnated, that's even better. Test the ball by rolling it to the cat. She may bite it and throw her legs around it while on her back, "gutting" it with her hind feet. This is what you want.

2. Lure her to the stairs. Start by dropping the ball gently from a few steps up, letting it roll down toward her for the "ambush."

3. Once she's on the stairs, go to the bottom and toss the ball up the stairs above the cat. She will learn to lie in wait for the ball to bounce over her. Cats often latch on to the ball, flopping down the stairs as they "kill" it and let off steam.

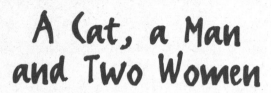

A Cat, a Man and Two Women

by Jun'ichiro Tanizaki

The shower passed over the roof again with its patter of rainfall, and then there was a sudden thud, of something bumping against the window. "The wind's come up. Oh, Lord." But just as the thought crossed her mind, something that seemed a bit too heavy for it to be the wind banged twice in succession against the glass, and Shinako heard a faint "meow" from somewhere. Surely not now, at this time of night . . . it couldn't be. . . . Startled, and thinking it must be her nerves, she strained her ears. "Meow." There it was again; and, right afterward, another bang against the window. Shinako jumped up and rushed to open the curtain. Now she clearly heard a "meow" from just outside;

and with another loud bang a shadowy black something flitted by. Was it true, then? . . . Could it really be so? . . . She knew that voice. She hadn't heard it even once during Lily's stay with her in this second-floor room, but she remembered it well from the days in Ashiya.

Hurriedly unlocking and opening the window, she leaned out and scanned the dark rooftop by what light there was from the overhead lamp in her room. For a moment everything was blackness. She supposed that Lily had climbed onto the small half-balcony with its railing and, meowing, knocked at the window. That would account for the banging sound and the fleeting black shadow a moment ago; but as soon as the

312

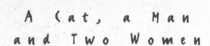

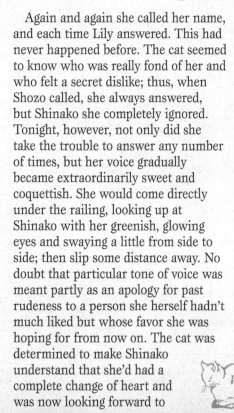

window was opened from inside, the cat must have run off somewhere.

"Lilyyy. . . ," Shinako called out into the darkness, taking care not to wake the couple downstairs. The roof tiles were wet and gleaming, so she had been right about the shower of a few minutes before; yet the clear night sky with its twinkling stars made it seem unreal now. On the broad, pitch-black flanks of Mt. Maya, which rose directly before her, the lights of the cable car had long since been extinguished, but some light could be seen in the hotel perched on the summit. Placing one knee on the low balcony, she leaned precariously out over the roof and called "Lilyyy . . ." again. There came a "meow" in reply, and two glowing eyes moved slowly across the tiles in Shinako's direction.

"Lily!"
"Meow."
"Lily!"
"Meow."

Again and again she called her name, and each time Lily answered. This had never happened before. The cat seemed to know who was really fond of her and who felt a secret dislike; thus, when Shozo called, she always answered, but Shinako she completely ignored. Tonight, however, not only did she take the trouble to answer any number of times, but her voice gradually became extraordinarily sweet and coquettish. She would come directly under the railing, looking up at Shinako with her greenish, glowing eyes and swaying a little from side to side; then slip some distance away. No doubt that particular tone of voice was meant partly as an apology for past rudeness to a person she herself hadn't much liked but whose favor she was hoping for from now on. The cat was determined to make Shinako understand that she'd had a complete change of heart and was now looking forward to

enjoying the lady's patronage and protection.

As for Shinako, she was as happy as a child at receiving such gentle, friendly responses from the cat for the very first time.

But, though she kept on calling to her, every attempt she made to catch hold of her ended in failure. She decided to move away from the window for a while to see what would happen, and, sure enough, Lily at last leapt nimbly into the room. Then, to Shinako's utter astonishment, she walked straight over to her as she sat on the bedding and placed her forepaws squarely in the woman's lap.

What could this mean? . . . As Shinako sat there amazed, Lily looked up at her with a gaze full of sadness and, pressing herself against her breast, pushed with her forehead at the collar of the woman's flannel nightgown. Shinako found herself rubbing her cheek against Lily's head; and before long the cat started licking at her chin, her ears, the tip of her nose, around her mouth—everywhere. Shinako had heard people say that when a cat was alone with its owner, it would sometimes kiss and rub its face against that person, showing its love in much the same way as humans do. Was this what they were talking about? When Shozo was off enjoying himself with Lily where no one could see them, was this what they were doing? Shinako smelled the peculiar, dusty odor of cat fur and felt all over her face the prickly, tickling friction of a cat's rough tongue against her skin. She felt a sudden surge of love and, crying "Lily," held her tightly in her arms.

The Mysterious Cat

by
Vachel
Lindsay

I saw a proud, mysterious cat,
I saw a proud, mysterious cat,
Too proud to catch a mouse or rat—
Mew, mew, mew.

But catnip she would eat, and purr,
But catnip she would eat, and purr,
And goldfish she did much prefer—
Mew, mew, mew.

I saw a cat—'twas but a dream,
I saw a cat—'twas but a dream,
Who scorned the slave that brought her cream—
Mew, mew, mew.

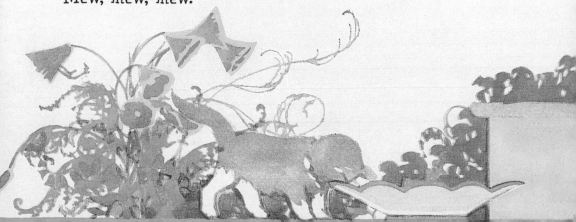

Unless the slave were dressed in style,
Unless the slave were dressed in style,
And knelt before her all the while—
Mew, mew, mew.

Did you ever hear of a thing like that?
Did you ever hear of a thing like that?
Oh, what a proud, mysterious cat.
Oh, what a proud, mysterious cat.
Oh, what a proud, mysterious cat.
Mew . . . mew . . . mew.

Shower Pong

This activity seems to be every cat's favorite, and it's especially good for a not uncommon behavioral problem: that unpleasant habit of peeing in the shower or bathtub. You've tried everything—cleaning and de-scenting, keeping plenty of clean litter boxes around—but Ms. Whiskers still thinks the shower is a giant litter box. This approach is called training an incompatible behavior, since cats will not normally pee where they play (or where they eat).

1. Open a package of Ping-Pong balls and start bouncing them around the shower or bath enclosure. If the noise doesn't draw feline fans, check your cats for a pulse! Lure them toward the bath-room with a ball.
2. Sit back and laugh. This activity is so much fun for cats, it's what's known as self-reinforcing. It doesn't require rewards, but you can sweeten the pot by giving treats to shy types for batting balls around.
3. Leave a couple of balls in the shower, and expect Pong to go on at any hour, once your cat gets the hang of it.
4. If your cat still has potty slipups, feed her in the tub exclusively for a few days. Animals will not toilet in an area they have learned to associate with food. If she does, suspect a bladder infection.

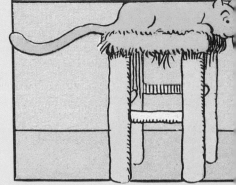

Heaven Sent

A cat dies and goes to heaven and meets God who says, "You've been good all these years. Anything you desire is yours." The cat thinks for a moment and replies, "All my life I've had to sleep on a hard wooden floor." Immediately, a large fluffy pillow appears.

A few days later, six mice die and go to heaven. God greets them at the gate with the same offer. They answer, "All of our lives we have been chased by cats, dogs, and women with brooms. We are tired of running." Immediately, six beautiful pairs of tiny roller skates appear.

About a week later, God stops by to see the cat and finds him snoozing on the pillow. He gently wakes the cat and asks, "How are things?" The cat stretches, yawns, and replies, "Oh, it's wonderful here. Those 'meals on wheels' you've been sending by are the best!"

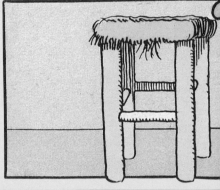

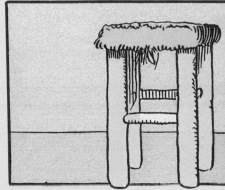

Feline Funnies

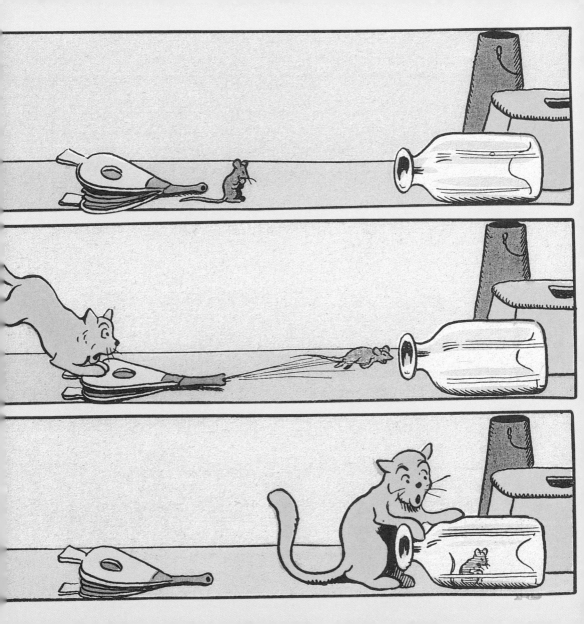

Sylvester's Health Biscuits

J ust like ours, your cat's sensitive skin gets dried out by winter's indoor heat. But what if Kitty keeps turning up his nose at that terrific liquid coat supplement you are proffering him with? Keep that glossy coat in shape by hiding it inside this delicious biscuit.

$^1/_2$ can tuna in oil, drained, with 2–4 tablespoons oil reserved

$^1/_2$ cup whole wheat flour

$^1/_2$ cup nonfat powdered milk

1 tablespoon liquid coat supplement or cod liver oil

1 egg, beaten

1 small jar chicken baby food (without onion powder)

1. Preheat the oven to 350°F.
2. In a large bowl, mash the tuna; add the flour and powdered milk. Mix thoroughly.
3. Stir in the coat supplement or oil, egg, and baby food. Blend in enough of the reserved tuna oil to make the dough easier to handle.
4. Flour your hands well and form the dough into small, flattened biscuits. Place on a greased cookie sheet.
5. Bake for 10–12 minutes, flipping the biscuits halfway through. Refrigerate in a sealed container for up to a week.

Makes about 8 dozen biscuits.

Pilling Your Cat

When it comes to giving meds, the do-it-before-she-knows-what-hit-her technique is best—cats hate to be restrained for long. Have irresistible treats handy as rewards.

Put the cat on a towel in your lap or on a counter. (The towel can be used to restrain her briefly if she claws.) Or simply lure her to you and give her a massage to relax her (page 276). Rub your cat's head reassuringly. Quickly open her mouth by squeezing the sides with one hand and pulling the lower jaw down with a finger. Push the pill into the throat from one side at the back—fast. Close her mouth—not too tightly—and hold her head up. Firmly stroke her throat and/or blow gently into her face to induce swallowing.

If she manages to spit the pill out, wait a few minutes and try again. If you continue to have trouble, hide the pill on your person and choose a time when your cat is unsuspecting. Your vet can give you a pill gun if necessary, but these often don't work well with small pills.

Kitty Beach

This installation comes from a cat friend with a large loft, a roomy bathroom, and two dignified, aging cats. His pets appreciated it by taking extended holidays there. Using a camera placed on a tripod and equipped with a timer, he managed to photograph them in some very "undignified" sleeping positions.

Vacation Station

lamp, towel, water bowl, plastic palm tree from a hobby store or novelty shop (you can also find mini props like sunglasses and picnic baskets), sheet of poster board about 8" x 14", scissors, X-Acto knife, large stick-on letters

1. Set up a heat lamp in your bathroom or other nondrafty, out-of-the-way area a few feet above the floor. Use a clamp light with a ceramic socket and metal shade from the hardware store—you also can rig it to a tripod or use a floor lamp. If you don't have a heat lamp, a regular incandescent bulb will do.

2. Place a thick, fluffy beach towel underneath the lamp. Arrange it around the drinking bowl to make this look like a pool. Add the plastic palm tree and other props to your set.

3. Cut out a piece of poster board and score it lightly crosswise in the center. Fold in half so that it will stand up. Use the display lettering to make a funny sign that reads KITTY BEACH, CATATONIC ISLAND, NO SWIMMING WITHOUT LIFEGUARD ON DUTY, or other humorous statement.

Vacation Album

camera, tripod, timer (optional)

1. Take snapshots of "vacationing" felines every half hour or other interval. It's most convenient to prefocus your camera and set it up

Kitty Beach

on a tripod so that all you have to do is click the shutter every so often. For the ultimate vacation album, use a self-timing device (from a photo supply store) that will take shots at set intervals over a 24-hour period. You will catch cats washing, "sunbathing," sleeping together, and probably even tussling over the warmest spot.

2. Print out and paste snapshots in a photo album with captions about their "vacation," or store photos in a digital album on your computer. E-mail them to friends!

The Islands

by Alice Adams

What does it mean to love an animal, a pet, in my case a cat, in the fierce, entire and unambivalent way that some of us do? I really want to know this. Does the cat (did the cat) represent some person, a parent or a child? some part of one's self? I don't think so—and none of the words or phrases that one uses for human connections sounds quite right: "crazy about," "really liked," "very fond of"—none of those describes how I felt and still feel about my cat. Many years ago, soon after we got the cat (her name was Pink), I went to Rome with my husband, Andrew, whom I really liked; I was crazy about Andrew, and very fond of him too. And I have a most vivid memory of lying awake in Rome, in the pretty bed in its deep alcove, in the nice small hotel near the

Borghese Gardens—lying there, so fortunate to be in Rome, with Andrew, and missing Pink, a small striped cat with no tail—missing Pink unbearably. Even blaming Andrew for having brought me there, although he loved her too, almost as much as I did. And now Pink has died, and I cannot accept or believe in her death, any more than I could believe in Rome. (Andrew also died, three years ago, but this is not his story.)

A couple of days after Pink died (this has all been recent), I went to Hawaii with a new friend, Slater. It had not been planned that way; I had known for months that Pink was slowly failing (she was nineteen), but I did not expect her to die. She just suddenly did, and then I went off to "the islands," as my old friend Zoe Pinkerton used to

call them, in her nasal, moneyed voice. I went to Hawaii as planned, which interfered with my proper mourning for Pink. I feel as though those islands interposed themselves between her death and me. When I needed to be alone, to absorb her death, I was over there with Slater. . . .

Andrew and I had acquired Pink from Zoe, a very rich alcoholic, at that time a new neighbor of ours in Berkeley. Having met Andrew down in his bookstore, she invited us to what turned out to be a very long Sunday lunch party, in her splendidly decked and viewed new Berkeley hills house. "Getting to know some of the least offensive neighbors," is how she probably thought of it. Her style was harsh, abrasive; anything-for-a-laugh was surely one of her mottoes, but she was pretty funny, fairly often. We saw her around when she first moved to Berkeley (from Ireland: a brief

experiment that had not worked out too well). And then she met Andrew in his store, and found that we were neighbors, and she invited us to her party, and Andrew fell in love with a beautiful cat. "The most beautiful cat I ever saw," he told Zoe, and she was, soft and silver, with great blue eyes. The mother of Pink.

"Well, you're in luck," Zoe told us. "That's Molly Bloom, and she just had five kittens. They're all in a box downstairs, in my bedroom, and you get to choose any one you want. It's your doorprize for being such a handsome couple." . . .

The one that Andrew had picked was gray striped, a tabby, with a stub of a tail, very large eyes and tall ears. I agreed that she was darling, how great it would be to have a cat again; our last cat, Lily, who was sweet and pretty but undistinguished, had died some years ago. And so Andrew and I went back upstairs and told Zoe, who was almost very drunk, that we wanted the one with no tail.

"Oh, Stubs," she rasped. "You don't have to take that one. What are you guys, some kind of Berkeley bleeding hearts? You can have a whole cat." And she laughed, delighted as always with her own wit.

No, we told her. We wanted that particular cat. We liked her best. . . .

"What a curious litter," I remarked to Andrew, walking home, up Marin to our considerably smaller house. "All different. Five different patterns of cat."

"Five fathers." Andrew had read a book about this, I could tell. Andrew read everything. "It's called multiple insemination, and occurs fairly often in cats. It's theoretically

possible in humans, but they haven't come across any instances." He laughed, really pleased with this lore.

"It's sure something to think about."

"Just don't." . . .

In a couple of weeks, then, Zoe called, and she came over with this tiny tailless kitten under her arm. A Saturday afternoon. Andrew was at home, puttering in the garden like the good Berkeley husband that he did not intend to be.

Zoe arrived in her purple suede pants and a vivid orange sweater (this picture is a little poignant; fairly soon after that the booze began to get the better of her legs, and she stopped taking walks at all). She held out a tiny kitten, all huge gray eyes and pointed ears. A kitten who took one look at us and began to

333

purr; she purred for several days, it seemed, as she walked all over our house and made it her own. This is absolutely the best place I've ever been, she seemed to say, and you are the greatest people—you are my people.

From the beginning, then, our connection with Pink seemed like a privilege; automatically we accorded her rights that poor Lily would never have aspired to.

She decided to sleep with us. In the middle of the night there came a light soft plop on our bed, which was low and wide, and then a small sound, *mmrrr*, a little announcement of her presence. "Littlest announcer," said Andrew, and we called her that, among her other names. Neither of us ever mentioned locking her out.

Several times in the night she would leave us and then return, each time with the same small sound, the littlest announcement.

In those days, the early days of Pink, I was doing a lot of freelance editing, for local small presses, which is to say that I spent many waking hours at my desk. Pink assessed my habits early on, and decided to make them her own; or perhaps she decided that she too was an editor. In any case she would come up to my lap, where she would sit, often looking up with something to say. She was in fact the only cat I have ever known with whom a sort of conversation was possible; we made sounds back and forth at each other, very politely, and though mine were mostly nonsense syllables, Pink seemed pleased.

Pink was her main name, about which Zoe Pinkerton was very happy. "Lordy, no one's ever named a cat for me before."

But Andrew and I used many other names for her. I had an idea that Pink liked a new name occasionally: maybe we all would? In any case we called her a lot of other, mostly P-starting names: Peppercorn, Pipsy Doodler, Poipu Beach. This last was a favorite place of Zoe's, when she went out to "the islands." Pink seemed to like all these names; she regarded us both with her great gray eyes—especially me; she was always mostly my cat.

I find that this is very hard, describing a long relationship with a cat. For one thing, there is not much change of feeling, on either side. The cat gets a little bigger, and you get older. Things happen to both of you, but mostly there is just continuation.

Worried about raccoons and Berkeley free-roaming dogs, we decided early on that Pink was to be a house cat, for good. She was not expendable. But Andrew and I liked to take weekend trips, and after she came to live with us we often took Pink along. She liked car travel right away; settled on the seat between us, she would join right in whenever we broke what had been a silence—not interrupting, just adding her own small voice, a sort of soft clear mew.

This must have been in the early 70s; we talked a lot about Nixon and Watergate. "Mew if you think he's guilty," Andrew would say to Pink, who always responded satisfactorily.

Sometimes, especially on summer trips, we would take Pink out for a semi-walk; our following Pink is what it usually amounted to, as she bounded into some meadow grass, with miniature leaps. Once, before I could stop her, she suddenly raced ahead—to a chipmunk. I was horrified. But then she raced back to me with the chipmunk in her mouth, and after a tiny shake she let him go,

and the chipmunk ran off, unscathed.
(Pink had what hunters call a soft
mouth. Of course she did.)

We went to Rome and I missed her,
very much; and we went off to the
Piazza Argentina and gave a lot of lire
to the very old woman there who was
feeding all those mangy, half-blind cats.
In honor of Pink.

I hope that I am not describing some
idealized "perfect" adorable cat, because
Pink was never that. She was entirely
herself, sometimes cross and always
independent. On the few occasions
when I swatted her (very gently), she
would hit me right back, a return swat
on the hand—though always with
sheathed claws.

I like to think that her long life
with us, and then just with
me, was a very happy one.
Her version, though, would
undoubtedly state that she
was perfectly happy until Black and
Brown moved in.

Another Berkeley lunch. A weekday,
and all the women present work, and
have very little time, and so this getting
together seems a rare treat. Our hostess,
a diminutive and brilliant art historian,
announces that her cat, Parsley, is
extremely pregnant. "Honestly, any
minute," she laughs, and this is clearly
true; the poor burdened cat, a brown
Burmese, comes into the room, heavy and
uncomfortable and restless. Searching.

A little later, in the midst of serving
our many—salad lunch, the hostess says
that the cat is actually having her kittens now, in the kitchen closet. We all
troop out into the kitchen to watch.

The first tiny sac-enclosed kitten to
barrel out is a black one, instantly vigorous, eager to stand up and get
on with her life. Then three more
come at intervals; it is hard to
make out their colors.

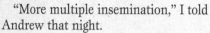

"More multiple insemination," I told Andrew that night.

"It must be rife in Berkeley, like everyone says."

"It was fascinating, watching them being born."

"I guess, if you like obstetrics."

A month or so later the art historian friend called with a very sad story: she had just been diagnosed as being very clearly allergic to cats. "I thought I wasn't feeling too well, but I never thought it could be the cats. I know you already have that marvelous Pink, but do you think—until I find someone to take them? Just the two that are left?"

Surprisingly, Andrew, when consulted, said, "Well, why not? Be entertain-ment for old Pink, she must be getting pretty bored with just us."

We did not consult Pink, who hated those cats on sight. But Andrew was right away crazy about them, especially the black one (maybe he had wanted a cat of his own?).

We called them, of course, Black and Brown. They were two Burmese females, or semi-Burmese, soon established in our house and seeming to believe that they lived there.

Black was (she is) the more interesting and aggressive of the two. And from the first she truly took to Pink, exhibiting the sort of clear affection that admits of no rebuff.

We had had Pink spayed as soon as she was old enough, after one quite miserable heat. And now Black and Brown seemed to come into heat consecutively, and to look to Pink for relief. She raged and scratched at them, as they, alternatively, squirmed and rubbed toward her. Especially Brown, who gave all the signs of a major passion for Pink. Furious, Pink seemed to be saying, Even if I were the tom cat that you long for, I would never look at you.

Black and Brown were spayed, and relations among the cats settled down to a much less luridly sexual pattern. Black and Brown both liked Pink and wished to be close to her, which she would almost never permit. She refused to eat with them, haughtily waiting at mealtimes until they were through.

It is easy for me to imagine Black and Brown as people, as women. Black would be a sculptor, I think, very strong, moving freely and widely through the world. Unmarried, no children. Whereas Brown would be a very sweet and pretty, rather silly woman, adored by her husband and sons.

But I do not imagine Pink as a person at all. I only see her as herself. A cat. . . .

Pink by now was in some cat equivalent to middle age. Still quite small, still playful, at times, she was almost always talkative.

She disliked Black and Brown, but sometimes I would find her nestled against one of them, usually Black, in sleep. I had a clear sense that I was not supposed to know about this occasional rapport, or whatever. Pink still came up to my lap as I worked, and she slept on our bed at night, which we had always forbidden Black and Brown to do.

We bought a new, somewhat larger house, further up in the hills. It had stairs, and the cats ran happily up and down, and they seemed to thrive, like elderly people who benefit from a new program of exercise.

Andrew got sick, a terrible swift-moving cancer that killed him within a year, and for a long time I did very little but grieve. I sometimes saw friends, and I tried to work. There was a lot to do about Andrew's bookstore, which I sold, but mostly I stayed at home with my cats, all of whom were now allowed to sleep with me, on that suddenly too-wide bed.

Pink at that time chose to get under the covers with me. In a peremptory way she would tap at my cheek or my forehead, demanding to be taken in. This would happen several times in the course of the night, which was not a great help to my already fragile pattern of sleep, but it never occurred to me to deny her. And I was always too embarrassed to mention this to my doctor, when I complained of lack of sleep.

And then after several years I met Slater, at a well-meaning friend's house. Although . . . I did not much like him at first, I was struck by his nice dark red hair, and by his extreme directness; Andrew had a tendency to be vague, it was sometimes hard to get at just what he meant. Not so with Slater,

who was very clear—immediately clear about the fact that he liked me a lot, and wanted us to spend time together. And so we became somewhat involved, Slater and I, despite certain temperamental obstacles, including the fact that he does not much like cats.

And eventually we began to plan a trip to Hawaii, where Slater had business to see to.

Pink as an old cat slept more and more, and her high-assed strut showed sometimes a slight arthritic creak. Her voice got appreciably louder; no longer a littlest announcer, her statements were loud and clear (I have to admit, it was not the most attractive sound). It seems possible that she was getting a little deaf. When I took her to the vet, a sympathetic, tall and handsome young Japanese woman, she always said, "She sure doesn't look her age—" at which both Pink and I preened.

The vet, Dr. Ino, greatly

admired the stripes below Pink's neck, on her breast, which looked like intricate necklaces. I admired them too (and so had Andrew).

Needless to say, the cats were perfectly trained to the sandbox, and very dainty in their habits. But at a certain point I began to notice small accidents around the house, from time to time. Especially when I had been away for a day or two. It seemed a punishment, cat turds in some dark corner. But it was hard to fix responsibility, and I decided to blame all three—and to take various measures like the installation of an upstairs sandbox, which helped. I did think that Pink was getting a little old for all those stairs.

Since she was an old cat I sometimes, though rarely, thought of the fact that Pink would die. Of course she would, eventually—although at times (bad times: the weeks and months around Andrew's illness and death) I melodramatically announced (more or less to myself) that Pink's death would be the one thing I could not bear. "Pink has promised to outlive me," I told several friends, and almost believed.

At times I even felt that we were the same person-cat, that we somehow inhabited each other. In a way I still do feel that—if I did not her loss would be truly unbearable.

I worried about her when I went away on trips. I would always come home, come into my house with some little apprehension that she might not be there. She was usually the last of the three cats to appear in the kitchen, where I stood confused among baggage, mail and phone messages. I would greet Black and Brown, and then begin to call her, "Pink, Pink?"—until, very diffident and proud, she

would stroll unhurriedly toward me, and I would sweep her up into my arms with foolish cries of relief, and of love. *Ah, my darling old Pink.*

As I have said, Slater did not particularly like cats; he had nothing against them, really, just a general indifference. He eventually developed a fondness for Brown, believing that she liked him too, but actually Brown is a whore among cats; she will purr and rub up against anyone who might feed her. Whereas Pink was always discriminating, in every way, and fussy. Slater complained that one of the cats deposited small turds on the bathmat in the room where he sometimes showered, and I am afraid that this was indeed old Pink, both angry and becoming incontinent. . . .

Two days before we were to go to Hawaii, in the morning Pink seemed disoriented, unsure when she was in her sandbox,

her feeding place. Also, she clearly had some bad intestinal disorder. She was very sick, but still in a way it seemed cruel to take her to the vet, whom I somehow knew could do nothing for her. However, at last I saw no alternative.

She (Dr. Ino, the admirable vet) found a large hard mass in Pink's stomach, almost certainly cancer. Inoperable. "I just can't reverse what's wrong with her," the doctor told me, with great sadness. And succinctness: I saw what she meant. I was so terribly torn, though: should I bring Pink home for a few more days, whatever was left to her—although she was so miserable, so embarrassed at her own condition?

I chose not to do that (although I still wonder, I still am torn). And I still cannot think of the last moments of Pink. Whose death I chose.

I wept on and off for a couple of days. I called some close friends who would have wanted to

343

know about Pink, I thought; they were all most supportively kind (most of my best friends love cats).

And then it was time to leave for Hawaii.

Sometimes, during those days of packing and then flying to Hawaii, I thought it odd that Pink was not more constantly on my mind, even odd that I did not weep more than I did. Now, though, looking back on that trip and its various aftermaths, I see that in fact I was thinking about Pink all that time, that she was totally in charge, as she always had been. . . .

I dreaded going home with no Pink to call out to, as I came in the door. And the actuality was nearly as bad as my imaginings of it: Black and Brown, lazy and affectionate, glad to see me. And no Pink, with her scolding *hauteur*, her long delayed yielding to my blandishments.

I had no good pictures of Pink, and to explain this odd fact I have to admit that I am very bad about snapshots; I have never devised a really good way of storing and keeping them, and tend rather to enclose any interesting ones in letters to people who might like them, to whom they would have some meaning. And to shove the others into drawers, among old letters and other unclassifiable mementos.

I began then to scour my house for Pink pictures, looking everywhere. In an album (Andrew and I put together a couple of albums, early on) I found a great many pictures of Pink as a tiny, tall-eared brand-new kitten, stalking across a padded window seat, hiding behind an oversized Boston fern—among all the other pictures from those days: Zoe Pinkerton, happy and smoking a long cigarette and almost drunk, wearing outrageous colors, on the deck of her house. And Andrew and I, young and very happy, silly, snapped by someone at a party. Andrew in his bookstore, horn-rimmed and quirky. Andrew uncharacteristically working in our garden. Andrew all over the place.

But no middle-year or recent pictures of Pink. I had in fact (I then remembered) sent the most recent shots of Pink to Zoe; it must have been just before she (Zoe) died, with a silly note about old survivors, something like that. It occurred to me to get in touch with Lucy, Zoe's daughter, to see if those pictures had turned up among Zoe's "effects," but knowing the chaos in which Zoe had always lived (and doubtless died) I decided that this would be tactless, unnecessary trouble. And I gave up looking for pictures.

Slater called yesterday to say that he is going back to Hawaii, a sudden trip. Business. . . . He certainly did not suggest that I come along, nor did he speak specifi-

cally of our getting together again, and I rather think that he, like me, has begun to wonder what we were doing together in the first place. It does seem to me that I was drawn to him for a very suspicious reason, his lack of resemblance to Andrew: why ever should I seek out the opposite of a person I truly loved?

I do look forward to some time alone now. I will think about Pink—I always feel her presence in my house, everywhere. Pink, stalking and severe, ears high. Pink, in my lap, raising her head with some small soft thing to say.

And maybe, since Black and Brown are getting fairly old now too, I will think about getting another new young cat. Maybe, with luck, a small gray partially Manx, with no tail at all, and beautiful necklaces.

On the death of a favorite cat,
drowned in a tub of goldfishes.

Ode

by
Thomas
Gray

'Twas on a lofty vase's side,
Where China's gayest art had dyed
   The azure flowers that blow;
Demurest of the tabby kind,
The pensive Selima, reclined,
   Gazed on the lake below.

Her conscious tail her joy declared;
The fair round face, the snowy beard,
   The velvet of her paws,
Her coat, that with the tortoise vies,
Her ears of jet, and emerald eyes,
   She saw, and purred applause.

Still had she gazed; but 'midst the tide
Two angel forms were seen to glide,
   The genii of the stream:
Their scaly armor's Tyrian hue
Through richest purple to the view
   Betrayed a golden gleam.

The hapless nymph with wonder saw:
A whisker first and then a claw,

347

With many an ardent wish,
She stretched in vain to reach the prize.
What female heart can gold despise?
    What cat's averse to fish?

Presumptuous maid! with looks intent
Again she stretched, again she bent,
    Nor knew the gulf between.
(Malignant Fate sat by and smiled)
The slippery verge her feet beguiled,
    She tumbled headlong in.

Eight times emerging from the flood
She mewed to every watery god,
    Some speedy aid to send.
No dolphin came, no Nereid stirred;
Nor cruel Tom, nor Susan heard;
    A favorite has no friend!

From hence, ye beauties, undeceived,
Know, one false step is ne'er retrieved,
    And be with caution bold.
Not all that tempts your wandering eyes
And heedless hearts, is lawful prize;
    Nor all that glisters, gold.

A cat's a cat and that's that.

—AMERICAN FOLK SAYING

ACKNOWLEDGMENTS

"Macavity" from OLD POSSUMS BOOKS OF PRACTICAL CATS, copyright 1939 by T.S. Eliot and renewed 1967 by Esme Valerie Eliot, reprinted by permission of Harcourt, Inc.

"Cat" from *Le Fleurs du mal* by Charles Baudelaire, Translated from the French by Richard Howard, Illustrations by Michael Mazur. Reprinted by permission of David R. Godine, Publisher, Inc. Copyright © 1982 by Charles Baudelaire, Translated from the French by Richard Howard, Illustrations by Michael Mazur.

"mehitabel and her kittens" from *archy and mehitabel* by Don Marquis. Copyright 1927 by Doubleday, a division of Bantam Doubleday Dell Publishing Group, Inc. Used by permission of Doubleday, a division of Bantam Doubleday Dell Publishing Group, Inc.

From *All Things Bright and Beautiful* by James Herriot. Reprinted by permission of Harold Ober Associates Incorporated. Copyright © 2004 by the author and reprinted by permission of St. Martin's Press, LLC.

"The Naming of Cats" from OLD POSSUM'S BOOK OF PRACTICAL CATS, copyright 1939 by T.S. Eliot and renewed 1967 by Esme Valerie Eliot, reprinted by permission of Harcourt, Inc.

"Cat" from SELECTED POEMS of Pablo Neruda, translated by Ben Belitt. Copyright © 1961 by Ben Belitt. Used by permission of Grove/Atlantic, Inc.

"The Cat that Walked by Himself" from *Just So Stories* by Rudyard Kipling. Published by Bantam Doubleday Dell Publishing Group, 1992.

From "Cat in the Rain." Reprinted with permission of Scribner, an imprint of Simon & Schuster Adult Publishing Group, from THE SHORT STORIES OF ERNEST HEMINGWAY by Ernest Hemingway. Copyright 1925 by Charles Scribner's Sons. Copyright renewed 1953 Ernest Hemingway.

"My Cat and I" by Roger McGough from *Watchwords* (Copyright © Roger McGough 1969) is reproduced by permission of PFD (www.pfd.co.uk) on behalf of Roger McGough.

From THE STORIES OF ALICE ADAMS by Alice Adams, copyright © 2002 by The Estate of Alice Adams Linenthal.

Used by permission of Alfred A. Knopf, a division of Random House.

"The Cat" Copyright © 1936 Ogden Nash, renewed. Reprinted by permission of Curtis Brown, Ltd.

"The Cats of Balthus" reprinted by permission of Louisiana State University Press from *The Language Student* by Bin Ramke. Copyright © 1986 by Bin Ramke.

Pages 260 and 329 reprinted with permission of Alfred Mainzer, Inc., Long Island City, NY.

From THE CAT WHO CAME FOR CHRISTMAS by Cleveland Amory. Copyright © 1987 by Cleveland Amory (Text); Copyright © 1987 Edith Allard (Illustrations). By permission of Little, Brown and Co., Inc.

John L'Heureux is the author of 17 books of poetry and fiction. He has taught English literature at Stanford University since 1973. 'The Thing About Cats' was first published in *The Atlantic Monthly*. Copyright © John L'Heureux 1971 by John L'Heureux. Used with permission of the author.

From *A Cat, a Man, and Two Women* by Jun'ichiro Tanizaki, translated by Paul McCarthy. Copyright © 1936 by Chuokoron-sha. English translation copyright © 1990 by Kodansha International. Reproduced by permission. All rights reserved.

Macmillan Publishing Co., Inc.: "The Mysterious Cat" from *Johnny Appleseed and Other Poems* by Vachel Lindsay, copyright © renewed 1942 by Eliabeth C. Lindsay in *Collected Poems*, Macmillan Publishing Co.

ILLUSTRATIONS

Pg. 1, 2, 244–245, 315–316: Katharine Sturges Dodge; pg. 17: B. Butler; pg. 18: M.A. Peart; Pg. 21, 28–29, 49, 100–101, 136, 192–193, 320–321: Benjamin Rabier; pg. 26: Pauli Ebner; pg. 27, 220, 260, 288–289, 308–309, 328–329: Alfred Manzier; pg. 33, 34, 35: Adolf Zábransky; pg. 44–45: Scott Langley; pg. 54, 205: Ruth E. Newton; pg. 55: Frances Brundage; pg. 57, 94–95: Kate Greenaway; pg. 61: E. Colombo; pg. 66, 69: Ann Anderson; pg. 89, 127: I.F. Young; pg. 99: Elsa Beslow; pg. 109: Helena Maguire; pg. 143, 252: Jessie Willcox Smith; pg. 144–145: Arthur Thiele; pg. 237: Fern Bisel Peat; p. 240–241: D. Merlin; pg. 303: Maude and Miska Petersham; pg. 318: Louis Wain.